The Mummifier's Daughter

A Novel In Ancient Egypt

Nathaniel Burns

Heiken Marketing

Copyright © 2014 by Heiken Marketing

All rights reserved. No part of this publication may be reproduced, distributed, or transmitted in any form or by any means, including photocopying, recording, or other electronic or mechanical methods, without the prior written permission of the publisher, except in the case of brief quotations embodied in critical reviews and certain other noncommercial uses permitted by copyright law. For permission requests, write to the publisher, addressed "Attention: Permissions Coordinator," at the address below.

Heiken Marketing
Schortens, Germany
heikenmarketing@gmail.com

Publisher's Note: This is a work of fiction. Names, characters, places, and incidents are a product of the author's imagination. Locales and public names are sometimes used for atmospheric purposes. Any resemblance to actual people, living or dead, or to businesses, companies, events, institutions, or locales is completely coincidental.

Edited (USA) by Joni Wilson

Other Books in This Series

Princess Of Egypt - The Mummifiers Daughter - Book 2

Curse of Anubis - The Mummifiers Daughter - Book 3

Secret of the 7th Scarab - The Mummifiers Daughter - Book 4

Chapter 1

Neti-Kerty made her way along the well-trodden dusty road, following the young boy who Shabaka had sent to fetch her. The sun had already set, casting a pale red glow over the city. The shepherds will be relieved, they will have a peaceful night, she thought as she followed the boy along the surprisingly empty street.

The young boy almost seemed to be skipping in front of her, his tanned skin glowing in the twilight, his movements rattling the bracelets and necklaces he wore: their bulk indicated that he was the eldest son in his family. His hair was shorn in the usual right sided side-lock, and his bare feet hardly seemed to touch the still hot road as he proceeded along it.

She could feel the heat of the road through the soles of her reed-woven sandals, as she followed him up another pathway and into the more affluent neighborhoods of Thebes.

The heat released by the mud-brick buildings, along with that from the roads, became oppressive on most days, even for those acclimatized to the searing Egyptian sun.

Even after sunset, it would take a while before the air cooled to more pleasant temperatures.

The scents of coriander flavored flatbread, beer and fried meat permeated the air around her as she made her way through the area where most of Thebes's merchants and traders lived. They would be entertaining guests, or possibly courting, unlike her, who had to tend to yet another of Shabaka's requests. Not that she minded, it just seemed that he was calling upon her more often of late.

She hastened to follow the boy, having lost her train of thought for a minute to the alluring scents surrounding her. She had not yet had time to eat, as she had spent most of the day assisting her father, who was aging and no longer as agile as he used to be, with the wadding of two bodies.

The work had rendered her skull itchy under her wig and her slip seemed stuck to her body as she moved. She had earlier excused herself from her parents' company and had been on her way to the river to bathe, wanting to wash away the stench of the dead and the salts they used, when the young boy had found her. And although she would not have wished to present herself in such a fashion, the boy had stressed the urgency of the summons and beckoned for her immediate departure.

The closer they came to the home of the deceased man, the more crowded the street became. Do these people not have homes to go to? she thought as the boy started to move into the crowd of onlookers, all shuffling to get a better view.

The scent of sweat, beer and dust filled the air, and had it not been for the fact that Neti was used to far more pungent human odors, and that her presence had been requested, she would have definitely turned away and returned home. The acidic scent lingered in her nose, as hot bodies brushed against her own.

A low and familiar murmur started up in the crowd as she moved along it, and soon enough those closest to her started parting. Many looked disdainfully at her and some even spat on the road as she passed them, ensuring they remained well clear as she continued unhindered through the remainder of the crowd.

The boy, without looking back, continued through the group and came to a halt at the doorway, where moments later Shabaka appeared to address him. The boy pointed in Neti's direction, and Shabaka turned his head to follow his indication, smiling slightly in greeting before turning his attention back to the boy and dismissing him.

Neti-Kerty smiled in return, and moved closer to the dark skinned Nubian. He had a better physique than other men his age, and had worked tirelessly to secure his position as Prefect of Thebes, a position authorized by their pharaoh Ramesses II himself.

Neti-Kerty and Shabaka shared a kinship, in that none in the town really held much regard for either of them.

"Evening Neti-Kerty," he greeted her as she arrived at the doorway, nodding his head and smiling warmly at her. 'Thank you for coming."

"Prefect Shabaka," she respectfully replied, lowering her gaze slightly. Her heart sped up at his smile. He was one of few who treated her as an equal.

"He has been dead for a while I am afraid – he is fat already," Shabaka said as they turned to enter the house. "And he stinks," he added as Neti-Kerty stepped past him and into the home.

The prevailing low hum in the crowd suddenly erupted, with an elderly woman contesting, "She should not be allowed in there: she will banish his soul to the underworld. The witch of the dead she is." Many of the onlookers around her nodded in agreement adding their voices to the accusation. "She is cursed, we do not want her here."

Shabaka looked out over the rowdy crowd before lifting his hand to silence them and asserting, "She is here by my request, and that is as we will leave it."

"You cursed Nubian, my father used to kill the likes of you. And he was right: no good comes from your kind," a man not far from the woman spoke up. "The pharaoh is crazy if he thinks your people would have any respect for our dead," the man concluded looking around him for support.

"Your kind will let that witch curse the soul of a trader," an elderly man shouted from the back.

Shabaka glanced out over the crowd before shaking his head slightly, then turned from them to enter the house, steeling himself against the stench of rotting flesh.

Inside, Neti-Kerty walked about the room. She glanced at things before finally coming to a standstill next to the body. Her breathing was distanced and shallow to avoid drawing in too much of the stench.

Shabaka watched as she made her way around the room again, her eyes scanning certain objects, before he spoke up. "There's no indication of blood having run from his body, and he is still young," he said, causing Neti to turn and look at him. "I don't know why he is dead."

Neti turned her attention back to the corpse, indicating, "His name is Nembetsen, the fourth son of Mindef the trader. He was one of the children that used to call me names," she added, addressing the man who was but a few years older than herself.

"You knew him then?" Shabaka asked her pointedly.

"Everyone knew him: he was one of the clever boys. He could outsmart anyone," she said as she crouched next to the body.

"Any idea what could have caused this?' Shabaka asked, drawing her attention to the room that was in slight disarray.

"He is too young to have died from problems with his body," Neti started as she looked more closely at the man's face, before reaching out to pull his wig from his head. Then turning her head to look at Shabaka, she continued, "But you knew that already, or you would not have sent for me."

"You have any idea what could have caused his death, or if he was even killed by someone?" Shabaka asked as he came to stand next to her.

Neti rose up from where she was crouched. "There's nothing on the table anymore, but it could have been removed or taken by a poor person. He is alone, not yet married, which would have made any meal he ate simple – bread, beer, with some meat." Neti's eyes swept about the room. "There is a dark mark on the floor, where he could have spilt his beer." She thrust out an arm, indicating a darkened patch on the floor next to the table. "However he has been dead for a while: his body is stiff. It will soften at some stage and make it easier to move and adjust him."

Neti then glanced at Shabaka. "I need to turn him over to have a look at his front."

"I'll help you with that," Shabaka said stepping closer, moving into position so that he could help her turn over the body. After completing this, he rose, grimacing, visibly put off by the stench and the appearance.

Neti looked the body over, taking note of the slight amount of blood having run from his mouth, checking the man's eyes.

Just then, Pa-Nasi, the Mayor of Thebes came into the room, demanding in a booming voice, "What is she doing here?" whilst pointing at Neti. "The citizens outside are in an uproar!"

Shabaka looked at the man and calmly replied, "I sent for her. I wanted her to have a look at the body. There is no wound and not enough blood loss for him to be dead."

"But you cannot have a woman in here, especially not her!" the mayor boomed, gesticulating wildly. "It is unheard of!" he screamed before covering his mouth, noticeably gagging at the stench.

"Neti works with bodies every day. There is very little she has not seen," Shabaka professed calmly.

"You think I do not know who she is?" the mayor countered loudly, his arms once again flying. "Or the old fool who is her father. He angers the gods with his actions." The mayor took a step towards Neti but then stepped back because of the odor, opting to remain near the doorway. "Who has ever heard of a female embalmer? She does not have the strength or purity to be considered as such," the man continued, waving his hand dismissively at her.

Neti simply ignored the man, and continued with her assessment.

"Look at the position of the body: already he is cursed," the mayor once again remonstrated. "He is stiff like a statue, his legs and arms sticking out awkwardly. He cannot be buried like that."

"What brings you here mayor," Shabaka asked, stepping between the mayor and Neti, effectively blocking the man's vision of her. "You do not usually concern yourself with the death of a trader?"

"I heard of the death of Mindef the trader's son from one of my footmen. Mindef is a good friend of mine," the mayor professed, trying to see past Shabaka to what Neti was doing.

Good source of suborn income you mean, Neti thought as she continued to assess the body.

"His father will be livid that you have a woman in here, especially her," the mayor scowled, before bitingly adding, "The witch of the dead."

"Just because you do not understand what she does, does not mean that it is sorcery," Shabaka countered the man.

"What else could it be? None of the other embalmers proclaim to have this skill," the mayor loudly decreed.

His words caused Neti to take a deep breath, before quietly replying, "Because their only concern is the money they receive for the body to be embalmed. They have no interests in the differences of its appearance."

"And she dares to talk back!" the man exclaimed. "You will not address me unless you are first addressed. Is that understood, woman?"

"Okay. So I won't tell you what happened," Neti said, rising from her position next to the body.

"And just what does your sorcery say happened?" the mayor challenged her. Neti regarded him for a moment before turning her attention to Shabaka.

"What I can tell you is that he was dead before sunrise today. He is still stiff and will soften soon," Neti began before turning toward the body. "From these marks here I can tell you he died with his face to the ground. All the blood lies on this side, meaning that when his heart stopped beating, everything sank down." She drew a finger close to the surface of the skin, indicating the marks on the body.

"You still have not told us how he died," the mayor challenged her.

Neti looked at the man for a moment before stepping slightly back from the body. "He was poisoned," she flatly stated, glaring at the man. "And I suspect it was in his food."

"There is no food here!" the mayor remonstrated once again, using wide gestures to demonstrate the absence of food in the room. "Do you see any?"

"It could have been removed," she calmly replied, turning her attention to Shabaka instead.

"From his position on the floor, it is safe to say that he was seated at the table, possibly eating. The poison in his food then took hold causing him to get up, but he stumbled and fell, knocking his beer to the floor..."

"Now there is beer too," the mayor inserted mordantly, cutting Neti short.

Neti took a deep breath to steady her temper before continuing. "When he fell to the ground, he bumped his head. There is a mark on his forehead. He also bit his tongue. See the blood from his mouth," she continued. "He then shook: this we can see from the ground around him. His Ba was fighting against his body dying," she concluded as she glanced at Shabaka.

"And just what poison would have been used?" the mayor asked with a scowl. "For there is none I know of that can cause this."

Neti regarded the man for a moment, not happy with his tone or his sudden change of attitude. Then, looking at Shabaka, who nodded his head slightly, she continued, "The dark areas of his eyes are enlarged, and the smell from him indicates that he has consumed either the purple death berry, or leaves of the plant."

"Ha!" the mayor snorted in response, before muttering, "No adult would consume those."

"That is why he has been murdered," Neti said, looking at Shabaka. "No man would willingly consume the purple death berry. It would have been put in his food or pressed and added to his beer. He would not risk damnation in the afterlife."

"And you claim to know this by looking at him," the mayor returned disbelievingly, adding, "you are a witch."

Just then, another man entered the house, halting in his tracks as he looked at those in the room. "What is that witch doing here?" he demanded, pointing at Neti. "It is enough that Nembetsen played around her as a child. I do not want her here. She must leave now, before she taints my brother's Ba," the man angrily spoke.

"She is here by my request," Shabaka firmly returned.

"She will curse him and my entire family in the afterlife. I want her out of here and another embalmer to take care of his body," the man insisted.

"She is not here to collect him for embalmment," Shabaka replied angrily.

"I do not care. The witch of the dead is not welcome in this house," the man shouted, pointing towards the door. "She will either leave now, or I shall throw her out."

"This is your brother's house. You cannot speak for the dead," Shabaka replied quietly.

"It is alright Shabaka. I am done here: he was murdered," Neti said, marching across to stand next to Shabaka.

"Ha! Murder! There are no signs of injury," Nembetsen's brother proclaimed.

Neti regarded the newcomer pointedly before calmly answering, "Your brother was a young man of good health. He has no wounds that are angered. He has no part that is broken or swollen with blood. His face is not blue from something stuck in his throat, yet he is dead." Noting how the man's eyes were enlarged, she continued, "His eyes are all seeing, wide open. It is one of the things the black death berries do." The man was about to speak when she continued, "The berries caused his Ba to leave his body. But he would not have chosen such a path himself, for he knows that his Ka would remain trapped, and, that at the weighing of the heart, he would be judged unworthy and his heart eaten by Ammit. No, he would not have wanted that," Neti said, shaking her head slightly. "There is no other cause that I can see. His skull is not fractured either," she finished, watching as the man gathered his thoughts.

"I do not believe you," the man countered. "Nembetsen had no enemies, none that wished him ill."

"I cannot tell you why he was murdered, only that he has been," said Neti. "Shabaka is charged with discovering why it was done."

Just then, Marelep entered the room and noticed Neti with the others. "Is he one of yours?" the man asked Neti as he pointed at the corpse. "I was told that I should collect the body."

"No, Marelep he is not one of ours," Neti addressed the embalmer. "Shabaka summoned me to look at the body, but you can take him. The family has already stated that I am not to touch him."

The man nodded his head in response and stepped closer to the body.

"You have no problem with her being close to the body?" the mayor disbelievingly asked the embalmer. "Surely Anibus will be offended at her presence."

"She is as good as the most seasoned of embalmers," Marelep said, stepping up to the body. "Her father has taught her everything he knows since her childhood. She understands the dead, knows their bodies, and respects them more than others who practice the trade." He quietly added, "He has been dead for a while already."

Neti simply nodded at that.

"Ha!" the mayor said as he moved next to Nembetsen's brother, who was overseeing his brother's body. "You embalmers charge too much for your work."

Maralep glanced towards the mayor, before speaking. "Each body takes two moons to prepare: embalming it is not done overnight. You have no respect for a craft that ensures a serene afterlife," he bitingly responded, before stressing, "our careful preparations ensure that your arm is not broken off in the process, and that you do not look like this man," he said pointing to the body before him. "Let's hope that the priest's prayers succeed in releasing his Ka," he concluded.

The mayor huffed in response, then waved a dismissive hand towards him before turning and taking his leave, mumbling slightly under his breath.

Shabaka looked at Neti for a moment, before speaking. "Come. I will walk home with you. I cannot have anyone harm you for coming at my request." Neti smiled at him and nodded her head slightly, before turning and stepping out of the house.

Most of the crowd had somewhat dispersed when they reappeared; however, some still remained and regarded her with disgust as she passed them. They quietly walked side by side through the streets, the heat slowly dissipating from the buildings as the darkness came to settle about them.

As they approached her parents' home, Neti spoke up. "I should invite you in for dinner, for I am certain you have not eaten."

Shabaka smiled sheepishly at that. "Your parents will not mind having me in their home?" he carefully asked.

"My parents are not like many of the others. To us all men are the same. The color of your skin does not determine the person you are, or how you should be treated."

"This from the only other person in Thebes who knows what it is like to be discriminated against," Shabaka quietly replied.

"I try not to let it bother me," Neti sincerely responded.

"It will not help you with finding a husband one day," Shabaka uncertainly returned.

"If he cannot accept me for who I am, then I do not want him," she firmly replied as they arrived at the house. "So you will break bread with us?" she asked as they halted at the door.

"If your parents will allow, then yes, I would like to break bread with you," he replied, indicating for her to proceed.

Neti loosened her shawl as she opened the door, immediately coming to a standstill on recognizing the copper tang of fresh blood in the air.

There is no reason for there to be blood in the house, and not that much that I can smell it so strongly, Neti thought as she stepped into the room. "Shabaka," she called quietly and heard the door creek behind her. "Something is wrong," she stated as she moved into the house. "Mother? Father? Where are you?" she called as she made her way to their room. Shabaka followed not far behind her.

She halted with a gasp as she came to her parents' door, the smell overwhelmingly strong. Her hands flew to cover her mouth as she gaped at the sight before her. Her heart pounded in her chest, her chest constricting, limiting her ability to freely breathe. She repeatedly gasped for air, at first unable to make a sound, as the tears started streaming down her cheeks. "No!" She finally managed to get the bewildering wail out.

Her wail brought Shabaka to the room, as Neti moved toward her parents lying in their blood-soaked bed. Noting the cruel and crude way their hearts had been cut from their bodies, she grasped her mother's shoulders, pulling her closer. "No, Mo, no! You can't go!" she cried, shaking her head and swaying back and forth whilst holding her mother. As the sobs escaped her she looked around the room, and noticing the blood patterns all over the walls:

"I will find those who did this to you, the ones who condemned you. I will find them." Looking toward her father, she promised, "I will make sure you receive your Akh."

Shabaka stood in the doorway, stunned, bearing witness to the scene before him: the young woman he had come to know so well over the past two seasons, holding on to her mother, tears streaming down her cheeks, as she vowed to find the ones who had done this to her parents.

In all his time as a prefect, he had never seen as much blood, never seen two bodies emptied of their hearts. Just then, he turned from the room, heading for the door, barely making it to the street before gagging dryly, thankful that he had not yet eaten. I will help her fulfill that promise to her parents, he told himself. The ones responsible will be found.

Her parents were talking to her, smiling, beckoning her to come toward them. The afternoon sun shone brightly, a gentle warm breeze filled the air. She was walking, walking, walking toward them. Why did they seem so far away? Why did she have to walk so far? They were closer now, she could almost touch them. Their eyes suddenly seemed lifeless, the light in them gone. She knew that look, spent many days a year looking at eyes like those. They were not those of her parents, her parents had vivid, expressive eyes: filled with love. These were dead. They held nothing, only a void. Then there was blood, so much blood. Its coppery scent filled the air, leaving an aftertaste in her mouth. It seemed to be everywhere, covering everything. She looked at her parents, their chests hacked open, their hearts gone, their bodies lying lifeless before her...

Neti jolted upright in her bed, a gut-wrenching scream emanated from her lips, robbing her of what little breath she had left. Her lungs burned in need of oxygen as she dropped her face into her palms, breathing harshly, shallowly: drawing much needed air into her oxygen deprived lungs. Her heart pounded in her chest. Her sweat drenched slip was twisted and clung irritably to her overheated skin, causing her to hastily tug it back into place.

A lingering smell of drying blood still permeated the air in the house. A reminder that it was not just a dream, a vivid and unwanted nightmare, but that her parents had been murdered: with their still-beating hearts ripped from their bodies.

Swallowing repeatedly against the sobs wanting to escape, she fought to contain her tears. Her eyes were swollen, tender: the saltiness of her tears burning her skin as they slipped past her closed lids, rendering her struggle futile. Murdered, but why? With their hearts cut out. Who could have done such a ghastly, gruesome act? Who would wish such evil on them? she thought.

The light from the full moon slipped through the narrow windows, situated close to the roof, illuminating her room in a pale glow. The quietness of the evening air and the unfamiliar solitude she found herself in, combined with the uncertainty of what daylight was likely to bring, left her body feeling sore, even numb.

In the wake of her grisly dreams and a rapidly escalating headache, Neti gave up on the idea of getting any rest and cast aside the light bed covers. She rose from the bed and made for the basin, drawing some water from a pitcher before splashing it on her face: wanting to alleviate the burning sensation around her eyes. Sighing audibly, she dried her face and made for the main living area, heading straight for the small table where she knew the lamp would be. She lit it and looked about the room, the low glow from the lamp was barely sufficient to light the far corners, it seemed barely sufficient to cast away the darkness that seemed to be encroaching on her. She debated whether to start a fire and make herself some tea, then decided against it.

Instead, she sat down next to the little table, bracing her elbows on her knees as she lowered her skull into her palms, groaning slightly as she applied pressure to its sides, hoping to elevate the pulsing ache that was starting to build.

She thought back to the previous evening: her arrival; the discovery and the multitude of events that had followed since then. Shabaka had been kind and supportive, notifying the required authorities and getting one of the town guards to help him move her parents' bodies to the Per-Nefer for preparation. He had eventually left the house after trying, unsuccessfully, to console her.

In the gray-light of predawn, a tall elderly man in long flowing robes made his way through the deserted streets and across the city. Suten Anu was the local tax scribe, and wise beyond his years.

Word had reached him of Neti-Kerty's parents' brutal slaughter, and he hastened toward their home, wanting to check up on their daughter. However the visit was not for personal reasons alone, for tucked under his robes was the rolled up papyrus scroll containing her father's will.

He had on several occasions pressed his friend to alter the will, never having been happy with its contents, and if he could have he would have altered it himself, to ensure that she was better taken care of.

He arrived at Neti's home just after sunrise and knocked on the door, patiently waiting for her to open it. He glanced down the road, knowing that it would not be long before the city stirred and news of Neti's parents started spreading, along with the usual slander that was associated with her name.

He heard the scraping of the door brace and watched as the door slowly receded inwards. Her face peered around it. Her eyes were red and swollen from crying; however she put on a brave face, like she had so often in her youth.

"Neti, you poor child," he gently said, opening his arms.

Neti slipped into them without hesitation and his arms closed round her, allowing her to bury her face in his chest. It was something she had done numerous times in her youth, especially when the other children had been merciless in their mockery. Even back then, it had been difficult to maintain a distance from her. She had crawled into his heart. She had been so willing, so eager to lean. Absorbing every bit of information she came across.

She had learnt to read and write faster than any of the boys in his tuition, owning an abstract mind that could distinguish interaction between objects and their effects on one another. Her spontaneity and willingness to help had set her apart from the other children, who had been more concerned with their social standing. And as he stood there holding her, with her shoulders shaking and her tears dampening his robe, his own heart wept, knowing that the tides were not in her favor.

He held her until she managed to regain her composure, allowing her to draw back when she was ready. She had never been one for making scenes, and looking about he noticed some of the citizens looking at them. Well, they will hear the news soon enough, he thought as she finally pulled back.

"Come in, come in," Neti hiccupped, stepping back to allow his entry into her home, and was about to close the door when she heard a familiar voice call her name from down the street. She turned her head in the direction of the sound and saw Thoth, limping slightly, coming toward her as fast as he could. They had been friends since childhood, with Thoth being a few years older than her. Their worlds were opposing in every possible aspect, with Thoth having been sold as a child slave and Neti being the daughter of an embalmer. His owner, Ma-Nefer, was a wealthy trader who owned many slaves.

"Neti!" Thoth urgently repeated when she turned in the doorway to look at Suten Anu, who was patiently waiting. The elderly man nodded his head, and Neti turned to gaze at Thoth as he came to a standstill in the doorway.

"Thoth!" she gasped, taking in the sight of Thoth's black eye and split lip. "He has beaten you again hasn't he?" Thoth sheepishly nodded his head and lowered his gaze.

Neti closed her hands, forming fists, as a bolt of anger shot through her. "Come in, Suten Anu has just arrived," she said, stepping back to allow him in, adding, "I'll see to your wounds."

"Greetings, Thoth," Suten Anu said with a tone of heaviness.

"Good morning, Sir," Thoth answered, lowering his head.

"I see your master has once again taken his petulance out on you," Suten Anu remarked, looking at the young man following Neti-Kerty toward the grass mat.

"Yes, Sir," Thoth replied with his gaze lowered.

"Sit down Thoth," Neti instructed, pointing to the one chair, and the bruised man was eager to obey her, taking the seat she had indicated.

Suten Anu also took a seat, watching as Neti drew water from the pitcher, seemingly having forgotten her own distress in the face of her friend's injuries. She returned to them and carefully applied the folded rag to his face, removing some of the blood while focusing her attention on the young man.

Once done, she lifted his hand and started clearing some blood from between his fingers. She rinsed the cloth in the bowl, her gaze remaining on the blood seeping from the cloth. But Suten Anu knew she was not as unperturbed as she seemed. He watched as her eyes closed and her body shuddered. Dropping the cloth, she stepped back from Thoth, breathing harshly.

"Neti!" Thoth called, getting up to follow her, his expression hurt.

"It's okay Thoth, I've just seen too much blood," Neti said holding her hands up, signaling to him to stop his advance on her.

Thoth looked at his hands, turning them over, before replying, "I should have washed them better before coming."

Thoth then looked at Neti before returning to his seat as she spoke up. "I can't help thinking that I'll wake up at any moment and find that this is all a nightmare – that the senselessness, the horror of it all will go away." She paused for a moment, taking a deep breath, before slowly asking, "Why would anyone do this?" Then she turned to look at Suten Anu. "They were honest people, humble people, you knew them," she insisted, before heatedly continuing, "they had no enemies, wished no one harm. Why them?"

Thoth's head lowered at that, his shoulders drooping. He then got up from his seat and walked over to Neti, opening his arms, intent on comforting her, but she immediately raised her hands to halt him and began irritably pacing the room.

"Have you noticed if anything has gone missing?" Suten Anu asked as he watched her clasping and unclasping her hands, her lips moving slightly but no sound coming from them.

Neti stopped and looked toward him, before replying, "I haven't gone through anything yet." She then glanced about the room, before saying, "Even if killing my parents was a part of a burglary, why would they have needed to cut out..." her voice hitched at that and she once again took a deep breath, slowly releasing it.

Once she appeared to have gathered herself she firmly decreed, "I swear by all that is sacred: I will find out those who murdered my parents and I will avenge their deaths. Nothing will stop me."

"Child, come and sit down beside me," Suten Anu calmly beckoned, drawing her over to where he was sitting. Neti took the seat next to him, sighing deeply whilst dropping her face into her palms.

Suten Anu reached out and took her hand in his whilst Thoth sat down across from them, his hands clasped together, his gaze fixed on the ground. He slowly started rocking back and forth slightly. His actions puzzled Suten Anu, however the scribe's concerns lay with Neti. "Your mother and father both loved you very much," Suten Anu began, causing Neti to look up at him.

"Yes," Neti answered, nodding her head slightly.

"What would they want you to do now, Neti? Certainly not spend all of your energy on seeking revenge? They would want you to do what is necessary in order to move forward with your life," he calmly stressed, watching as Neti lifted her head, the persistent spark of her nature once again coming to the fore, as she spoke up. "But I have to find out who did this, and why they did this! My parents will be condemned to the underworld if their hearts are not found and returned to them."

"This I understand, my dear child. All in good time. There are many things that need to be addressed at times like these, therefore you will require patience. But for now, you must think about today, and the things that need to be done today."

Neti thought things over, giving Suten Anu the opportunity to look toward Thoth. He could feel the frown forming on his forehead as the young man continued to rock backwards and forwards. *Does he know? Is that the reason for his strange behavior? He has always been partial to Neti. Her and her parents were the only people who treated him well, could that man be as cruel as to taunt him with it,* the scribe thought, before speaking up. "Thoth, you should get going, Ma-Nefer is certain to whip you until you bleed if you are not on your post." He watched as the slave continued to rock, shaking his head.

"I should start cleaning up the blood," Neti said, causing Suten Anu to turn towards her.

"In good time my dear, there are more pressing matters," he advised, patting her hand softly.

"More pressing?' Neti asked, her brow furrowing slightly.

"Yes there is the matter of your parents' will," Suten Anu said, reaching under his cloak and extracting the papyrus scroll. "My footman will have gone to inform all those mentioned of its reading, they will be here shortly."

Neti looked at him pointedly, tilting her head faintly, "There is something you are not telling me," she stated, before adding, "and it is not good news."

"I am afraid it is not, but whatever happens, know that I will help you wherever I can." Suten Anu watched as she withdrew slightly, then added, "Now go get ready, the others will be here soon. I will let them in."

Neti got up from her seat, her movement caused Thoth to look up and also start to rise. "No Thoth, you stay here," Suten Anu said reaching for the man's arm. Thoth wailed as the scribe's hand curved round his arm, jerking hard then falling back and knocking over the chair, before landing on the ground.

Suten Anu held up his hands, palms forward, to calm the man, "Relax Thoth, she is just going to change, Neti will be back soon." The young slave looked at him and then moved away, before getting up from the floor and picking up the chair, obviously intent on keeping it between them.

What has that man done to you? Suten Anu thought. How much have you endured under his cruel hand to react like this?

Just then a knock sounded at the door and Suten Anu looked towards it, before glancing back at Thoth, holding up his hand as he spoke. "Stay there, I'm going to go open the door." He then stepped from the mat to open the door, nodding his head in greeting as Asim, Neti's father's long time friend and fellow embalmer made to enter the house. "Asim it is good of you to come on such short notice," the scribe spoke, beckoning for the man to enter.

"It is indeed sad times," the elderly man professed as he stepped past the scribe, nervously glancing about, before asking, "How's Neti?"

"She is as well as to be expected," Suten Anu answered, making to close the door when a firm voice stopped him, "just a moment."

The scribe turned to look at the tall Nubian, and nodded his head in greeting, "Shabaka, I am glad you could make it."

"It is the least I can do, considering the aid she has given me," the man calmly spoke.

"You will act as a witness for the reading?" Suten Anu asked, stepping out of the way to allow the man through.

"Yes," the man affirmed, slipping past him and into the room.

A few others arrived, before Neti appeared from her room. She greeted all those present and took a seat. Suten Anu watched as Shabaka approached her, and then sat down next to her. There had been rumors of the man's partiality toward her, and although he had never before seen the two of them together, Shabaka's attentions, although not obvious, were encouraging. He wondered if there was any chance that Neti returned them. He watched as Thoth came to stand behind Neti, his dislike of Shabaka's attentions and proximity to the young woman strongly evident.

Suten Anu also sat down and pulled out the papyrus scroll from beneath his cloak. There was a beneficiary still missing, however Suten Anu had no intention on waiting on the man, as he already knew what he stood to gain. He unrolled the scroll before drawing everyone's attention and started to read through the details. The majority was requisite legal jargon that dealt with the payments of debts, her parents' funeral arrangements, and the completion of any bodies still in need of anointing and wrapping: Asim was charged with this.

Suten Anu then halted for a moment, glancing about the room, drawing in a deep breath. His heart pounded in his chest as he looked down at the remaining words on the scroll.

"To our daughter, I leave the tools of my trade, so that she can continue the family tradition on receiving her certification. In the event of our death preceding that of her marriage, or a suitable engagement, we are bound by the agreement undertaken with Ma-Nefer that she is to become his wife, as a guarantee or compensation for the payment of goods provided, or payment of debts still owing to him," Suten Anu halted when everyone gasped.

"What!" Neti exclaimed in utter disbelief. "My parents would not have done that," she protested, looking towards Suten Anu, "There has to be some kind of a mistake."

"I'm afraid not, your father had me oversee the arrangement," the elderly scribe maintained.

"But I cannot marry him!" she retorted. "How can this be?"

"Ma-Nefer demanded a security on goods your father ordered, and your father had none to offer. Ma-Nefer was also not interested in your home, so he insisted that your father place you up as a security. At the time, there was no reason to believe that your father would not make the payments, and the goods were needed for your father's practice," Suten Anu explained.

"So I am to marry him?" she asked, shaking her head. I cannot marry that man: he has the face of a toad and the manners of a pig. He is cruel, malicious. There is nothing to love or honor. I could not even like him if my life depended upon it.

"There are alternative provisions made," Suten Anu countered, "however they may not be feasible."

"Death and eternal damnation would be better than marrying that man," she complained. The room was silent, with Thoth and the others rendered speechless.

Just then the door burst open, with Ma-Nefer taking up almost the entirety of its width.

"You," the man proclaimed, pointing at Thoth, "get me a chair."

Thoth leapt up from where he was sitting, collecting a chair and pusillanimously approached the man, placing the chair for him to sit.

Ma-Nefer backhanded Thoth, proclaiming, "You are away from your post, I will see to you later." He took a seat, the wood creaking under the strain.

"It is not yet working time," one of the men in the room spoke up, causing Ma-Nefer to turn toward him as he boomed, "You want to tell me what to do with my property?" The other man shook his head in response, "It is already enough that you have started without me."

"We were just finishing up," Suten Anu replied, rolling up the papyrus scroll.

"Oh well then they know," the man said rising from his chair, "I will be gracious, in that I will allow for the settlement of the estate, before disclosing on what is mine," he looked around the room before glaring at Neti, and stating, "This place had better be fit for habitation by then. I intend to lease it out." He turned from the room and marched toward the door. "Come you useless piece of flesh," he barked at Thoth, "get going." Thoth jolted forward and through the doorway, with Ma-Nefer following in his wake.

The door remained open after the man's departure, with everyone gawking in disbelief, before turning their attention towards Neti. Her heart pounded in her chest, the bile rising from her stomach at the thought. I would rather die, she thought turning to Suten Anu, and asking, "What are the alternatives?"

Suten Anu did not even unroll the scroll as he turned to look at her, "In the event of your marriage prior to the death of your parents, whatever outstanding funds would have been payable by you and your husband."

"But I am not married, therefore it does not apply," Neti quickly dismissed.

"The other was: that in the event of you already being licensed, you would have the option to pay back whatever amount is outstanding, and as such buy your way out of the marriage."

"I have not yet received my license," Neti replied dejectedly, "we only recently applied for it."

"Of that I am aware," Suten Anu replied. "I will stall proceedings as much as I can, in hope that it is granted, however your father's estate was not large, therefore there would not be many reasons for delay."

"I understand," Neti dejectedly replied.

"It's time for me to go to my office now, Neti. You must stay focused on what needs to be done." Neti nodded her head in response, before seeing out her guests.

Chapter 2

Neti closed the door after her last guest's departure. Turning her back she braced herself against it as a disconsolate sigh escaped her lips, causing her shoulders to sag slightly. Her hands clenched into fists as she fought against the heavy sensation that once again came to settle over her heart. Her stomach grumbled lowly, reminding her that she had not eaten anything since the day before: the events of the previous evening having robbed her of her appetite.

Gathering her verve she righted herself and made for the kitchen, only to falter on entering it, uncertain of the food stores available.

Her mother had always seen to their meals, had always ensured that there was enough grain and vegetables in the house; although proficient in cooking, Neti had never needed to manage the kitchen.

She looked over the room, her gaze landing on the pottery pot situated next to the oven, the one in which her mother always stored extra flatbread, and made for it.

Opening the lid, she reached into it, relieved when her hand came into contact with some bread. She drew out a piece and closed the jar again, turning for the storage area in search of some fruit, at the same time confirming the grain level. She would have to go to the market place soon, a chore she had never been partial to, just the thought of the milling bodies, the looks and insults habitually flung her way was enough to put her off it entirely. With a slight shake of the head she placed the bread and fig on a plate before reaching for a goblet, filling it with beer. She then settled on the woven mat, crossing her legs and placing her plate on her lap like she had as a child, and started on her meal.

Her mind started processing everything she needed to do, whilst chewing on her bread, a heavy sigh escaping her at the thought of cleaning her parents' room. She shook her head as a heavy sensation over her heart intensified.

Once done she cleaned her plate and goblet, and returned them to their respective places, before returning to the main living area and onto her parents' bedroom. She steeled herself by drawing in a deep breath before entering the bloody room, her stomach churning markedly; leaving her to wonder if it had been such a good idea to have breakfast before starting. However, she knew that very little ever got done on an empty stomach.

The sight of their blood no longer turned her stomach as much as it had the night before. The years assisting her father had desensitized her to such things. The red mud-brick walls, where the castoff blood had been absorbed, were stained a darker shade of brown, with most of the blood having coagulated already. She looked at the walls as she stepped further into the room, knowing that they would take time to scrape and repair.

She looked about the room, indecisive of where to start, when her gaze landed on the bed and the blood-soaked sheets. She gave a slight shake of the head at the thought of burning them, knowing that the blood would not wash out of the cotton fibers. She moved forward, reaching for the sheets, when her movement suddenly faltered, remembering her father informing her of a small purse he held in case of emergencies. She stepped a little away from the bed, trying to remember where he had told her he put it.

Her gaze landed on the small pedestal next to the bed; her thoughts however wandered elsewhere – on whether, she would find anything – on whether whoever had killed them would have taken the money. She knelt beside the bed and reached under it, feeling if there was anything there. Her hand brushed against a coarse cloth which she gripped and pulled. It came loose fairly easily; the jangling of coins confirming that it was the purse her father kept. Holding it in her hand, she sat back on her haunches perplexedly looking at it, unable to understand why someone would have left it, before opening it to look inside. There was a small amount of coins, enough to tide her over for a while.

She closed the small pouch before rising from her place and glancing at the other side of the bed, knowing her mother's jewelry would be there. She moved over to it, lifting the top of her clothes chest, moving the wigs and dresses aside as she picked up the wooden box. Lifting the lid to ascertain the contents, her brow furrowed when everything appeared to be there. Their presence confirming that whoever had entered their home had been intent on killing her parents for whatever reason. She placed the coins in the jewelry box, returning the lid, before leaving their room.

She placed the box on the stool before moving the small table that housed the Senet game, bending to move the floor covering it stood on, and revealing a small dug out. She lifted the wooden cover before turning to the stool to take up the box and place it in the small area; she then closed it up again and returned the table to its place, resetting the Senet pieces.

She returned to the room, going to the side of the bed, this time gripping the sheets and pulling them from the bed and bunching them together, before turning from the room and exiting the house.

The people walking along the street looked at her disdainfully. Many followed her progress, some having moved to the other side of the road as she approached. She made her way to the city's reuse site: the smoke already rising from the burning pits as men went about reducing the city's waste to ash for the masons to use in their mud-bricks.

The men were lugging some broken furniture into the pit when Neti arrived. She approached them and they made no attempt to halt her progress, some even moving out of the way to allow her access. She stopped at the pit's edge, where she first dropped the bundle of linen to the ground, before tugging each item out separately and dropping it into the pit.

She watched as the fabric first darkened from the heat, before the flames licked at it. The smoke lifting from the material set her into a trance as the white fabric was consumed...

"Come Neti, bring me that bolt of cloth, and I will make you a slip." Her mother's voice sounded in her mind. She had been six, and finally old enough for clothes. She had watched as her mother measured and cut the fabric, drawing it together. She knew her mom was good at making clothes, many of the women often came to her for slips and sashes, and Neti had pleaded for her own. Having wished the time could pass quicker, until she was considered old enough for clothes...

"Come Neti, it is time to go!" Her mother spoke up walking towards the door. Neti saw the bundle of fabric and knew her mother was going to go do washing. She jumped up from the floor, where she had been drawing with a stick in the sand – practicing the symbols Suten Anu had shown her. She ran ahead, skipping and singing as they walked down to the river; she always picked flowers whilst her mother did the washing.

"Throw those away my dear, they are evil," her mother firmly stated.

"But they are so beautiful," Neti said, looking at the off-pink flowers she held.

"They are the flowers of the black death berry, they are evil. Leave them be, and go wash your hands, we have to collect herbs for your father," her mother firmly spoke. Neti looked at the flowers before dropping them on the ground.

"You see that plant there, with the yellow flowers?" Her mother spoke up pointing to the plant in question, "That is the one we give to women who have trouble with milk for their babies."

"But all women have milk for their babies," an older Neti replied.

"Yes dear, but some do not have enough, and the baby becomes weak."

"What about that one mamma?"

"The white one?" her mother asked, looking in the direction Neti was pointing. "Yes, that is also a good plant. You use the leaves and twigs from it. We grind them into a paste to put on angry wounds," her mother added.

"And that one? You always put it in our food."

"That one makes your skin beautiful."

Neti swallowed against the burning sensation in the back of her eyes; fighting back the tears as the flames devoured the fabric. "No my girl, roll it the other way. The little pockets must be on the outside."

"Why do you put pockets on daddy's bandages? None of the other embalmers do it."

"It keeps the amulets in place when he wraps them, so they don't fall out when the body is moved," her mother calmly answered her.

"Then why don't the others do it as well?" Neti asked looking towards her mother, who was working on a new bed cover for her parents' bed.

"Because they make their own bandages and it takes time," her mother replied, before going back to work.

Neti felt the hot tears run down her cheeks, the flames engulfing that same bed cover. She swallowed repeatedly, fighting to keep the sobs down. Turning to look about her, she noticed the men staring in her direction. She turned and ran to the only place she had ever felt safe from others: home.

She burst into the house, looking about the room before dropping sobbing to the ground: How could they? How could they leave me here on my own? To that man, no he's not a man he's a pig! Neti picked up a small pot and flung it across the room. It struck the far wall, shattering into pieces: I refuse to marry him. I will not. You were supposed to be at my wedding, mom. You were going to make my dress. This is not fair! This is not right! You were going to help me with my children. Why did you go? Why did you leave? Neti's shoulders drooped, then started shaking as she allowed the sobs to escape, unchecked.

A while later Neti gathered herself off the floor, feeling weak and spent, before returning to the kitchen, dragging her heels as she made for the corner where her father had kept all the tools.

She selected the scraper and returned to their bedroom, feebly setting about scraping the walls, chipping away the blood infused plaster.

It was one of the skills her father had taught her, having always professed that: "Those who have many skills, have naught trouble that could be solved."

A few hours later she swept up the scrapings and placed them in a pottery pot. She then entered the main living area to pick up the broken shards of the pot she had earlier thrown, following which she returned to the dump to empty out the pot before making for the masons' area.

"What do you want, witch?" The one man asked, disdainfully looking her over.

"I need some mud for the walls of my home," Neti firmly said, meeting the man's stare.

"Be off with you, we don't want the likes of you here," the man snarled, waving a hand dismissively at her.

"Yes, we have no wish to be cursed," one of the others spat, before they all turned from her to continue their work. All but a younger man, who looked her over, "Is it true that you talk to the dead?" he asked, inclining his head slightly.

Neti drew in a deep breath before answering, "No. I do not speak to the dead. If I could I would ask my parents who killed them," she bitingly returned, then started to turn from him. "I do not have time for this; I'll go find some building mud elsewhere."

"Then why do they call you to look at the bodies?" the young man asked, causing Neti to turn her head to look at him.

"Why do you ask?" she questioned, somewhat irritated.

"I just want to know why everyone seems so scared of you. To me you just look like a girl."

Neti turned to regard him, tilting her head slightly, before nodding her head. "They call me because I understand bodies, how long they have been dead, what could have caused their deaths, and if they have been moved after having died. It helps the guard find those who murdered them, if they were murdered."

"So you do not hear anyone speak to you?" he asked, causing Neti's heart to start pounding, she had had so many mocking sessions start like that.

"No," she firmly answered.

"Here," the young man said indicating to her to hold her pot out.

Neti did as he asked, and he dropped some of the muddy mixture into it.

"Why?" Neti asked confused, looking at the contents.

"You're nothing but a woman who has learnt about the dead, there is nothing scary in that," the man remarked, "so there is no reason why I cannot help you."

Neti looked at him, and nodded her head in response. "I will bring you some bread and fruit once I have been to the market."

"Thank you," the man replied, acknowledging her.

Neti returned home and went to work on the walls before wiping the blood from the wooden furniture and finally sweeping the floor. Once done, she looked out over the room, her heart still heavy as she resolved to make new linen for the bed. She turned from the room, her body felt hot and sticky. The dirt having ingrained itself between her clothes and skin, left her feeling itchy and irritable. She looked down at her wrap, noting the stains and dirt streaks on it, knowing she would have to wash it, and returned to her room. Drawing out another slip from her clothing chest, she looked it over before gathering up her bath necessities and making her way down to the river.

Neti returned home and hung the recently washed slip up to dry, scrutinizing it in the light and then sighing, not understanding how her mother had always managed to get their clothes clean. She swallowed against the lump that formed in her throat, and the sudden ache in the back of it that followed. Instead she returned inside and moved the Sinet game, drawing the jewelry box from its confines, then sat at the table. She pulled out the coins, placing them to one side, and then carefully unpacked the jewelry, going over each piece before feeling her brow furrow when she noticed her mother's favorite amulet was missing; then she went through the contents once again, trying to remember if it had been around her mother's neck the previous evening, but failing to do so.. She shook her head at the thought that the murderer could have taken it; knowing that to one with such intentions, a purity of heart amulet would be worthless.

Neti carefully placed all of the jewelry back into the box before pulling the small pouch of coins closer. Opening it, she emptied it out onto the small table, counting them, before gathering them up again and returning them to the pouch, all but one.

Drawing in a deep breath and swallowing against the pain in the back of her throat, she returned the coins to the chest, then placed the chest back in the dugout before righting the room. She had just managed to finish when a knock sounded at the door. Sighing in dejection, not wanting more visitors, she got up and made to answer, checking to see if her wig was on properly.

Opening the door revealed Shabaka, and a slight smile tugged at the corners of her mouth when he spoke up. "I just came to see how you're doing."

"Come in," Neti invited, stepping back to allow him entry.

He turned to look at her, tipping his head slightly before asking, "Are you okay?"

Neti looked at him for a moment before dropping her gaze to the floor and shaking her head, "Not really." She moved from him, before lifting her head and asking, "Would you like something to drink? I still have to go and draw water but I can offer you some wine or beer."

"I'm fine thank you. I was hoping to talk to you about your parents' death," he softly spoke up, causing Neti to turn and look at him.

"Please sit," she invited, indicating the chairs, "what do you need to know?"

"Is there any possibility that your father could have had a misunderstanding with another embalmer, or that anyone could wish him dead?" Shabaka asked as he sat down.

Neti thought about it for a short while before shaking her head, "No. None that I can think of. The embalmers respect one another, there are at times more bodies than they have space or time for, so they often help each other out," she concluded before also sitting down.

"So you don't think that their murder could in any way have been related to his business?"

"No. Why do you ask?"

"I had most of the local embalmers brought in today, and they were all very forthcoming. Most of them had valid alibis and professed that they would not wish your father any harm." Shabaka halted for a moment, looking pointedly at her before continuing. "But there was one, Asim. He was here earlier today for the reading. He seemed nervous, very much like he had something to hide. He also did not want to look me in the eye when I asked him about matters."

Neti shook her head. "I would not be concerned about Asim or his wife Tei-ka. They were good friends of my parents, and often used to visit us. I often spent a lot of time as a child with them, when my parents had to be somewhere. Their son died when he was very young. My mother always said that Tei-ka's pain was so great that they could not have more children because of it. No, I do not think it is them, Asim taught me much of what I know, he and my father often worked together when there were too many bodies to embalm. He would not wish ill on my family."

"I have nowhere else to turn to," Shabaka stated, frustrated. "I sometimes wish this was easier. The mayor will possibly notify the Vizier and the city gates will be closed."

"That will not bode well for trade," Neti thoughtfully replied.

"No it does not," Shabaka concurred, "but three murders in two days is not to be taken lightly. And unless I find something soon, I have nowhere to go. Have you had chance to check if anything has been taken?"

Neti nodded her head in reply, "Yes, there has."

"Anything that could identify a person?" Shabaka hopefully asked.

Neti shook her head, "My mother's purity of heart amulet is missing. My father gave it to her a while back, she always wore it."

"And you think whoever did it might have taken it?"

"It could have been on my mother's neck the other night, I did not check for it."

"Then it would be with Asim?" Shabaka professed.

"Possibly," Neti concurred, "I don't really need it. I would rather for her to be buried with it."

"We can go see them in the morning, if you do not mind accompanying me, I have some questions for Asim, and speaking with his wife may also help."

"I don't mind," Neti sincerely replied.

Shabaka looked at her for a moment, before reaching out to touch her hand. Heat coursed up her arm at the contact, causing her to look at him in question.

"What are you going to do about Ma-Nefer? He is not a suitable match for you."

Neti looked away before replying, "I'm going to Suten Anu tomorrow to find out the state of my father's affairs, I'm hoping that I can pay off all the debts and so buy my way out of the marriage."

"And if you can't?" Shabaka insisted, squeezing her hand slightly.

"Then I will have to find another way. I cannot marry such a man."

"What about your father's provision?"

Neti looked at him once again before shaking her head, demurely answering, "I do not have a suitable offer in marriage. I do not even know of anyone who would be interested. Also, I cannot simply accept one man because it will prevent me from marrying another. I could never ask that of anyone. I have seen how many fight. I would want a relationship like my parents had, they were happy. It is not something to be entered into lightly, even if someone was interested."

"I see. So you would not consider my offer if I were to extend it," Shabaka hesitantly replied.

Neti looked at him in shock, "We barely know one another. I could not ask of you to do such a thing. We cannot get to know one another in a matter of days, in order to stop the marriage. And Ma-Nefer is cruel enough to enforce his intentions if I do not get married within that time. No, I will not allow for you to do such a thing. I will go see Suten-Anu in the morning and discuss my options with him."

Early the following morning, Neti-Kerty made her way through the rapidly warming streets to Suten Anu's office. Most of the citizens were still eating breakfast, with many of the children already out on errands. She watched as a boy passed by, carrying an urn of water and smiling warmly at her. A dog tagged along behind him, sniffing nooks and crannies for something to chase, before scampering to catch up.

On her arrival at Suten Anu's office, one of his footmen nodded in greeting and indicated that she could enter.

"Good morning, Suten," Neti warmly greeted, as she approached his desk.

"Neti, my dear girl, what a lovely surprise. I had not thought I would see you today," he said rising from his seat and grasping her shoulders, before kissing both of her cheeks. "You look tired," he stated, holding her from him slightly.

"I have not slept well since my parents…" Neti allowed the remainder of the sentence to trail off, her voice carrying a disconsolate quality.

"Ah yes, it is to be understood," Suten said stepping from her and returning to his desk. "So, dear child, what brings you to my door?"

"I came to talk to you about my parents' property," Neti spoke up, lacing her fingers slightly and visibly swallowing.

"What about it?" Suten asked looking at her, his head tilting slightly.

"I want to know if it would be possible to buy myself out of this marriage with Ma-Nefer," Neti hesitantly started. "I really do not want to marry him: I would rather live with nothing."

"I had a look at your father's matters late last night," Suten Anu started before looking through a group of scrolls. "Now where did I put that scroll?" he muttered, before selecting one and opening it, exclaiming, "Ah, yes! Here we go," he said, looking up and smiling at her, "You must understand that I'm not finalizing anything until we know when your papers will arrive. There are taxes due to the pharaoh, however not too great an amount. Your father's estate is big enough to cover those, and possibly most of the debt owing Ma-Nefer."

"Then I would like for that to be done," Neti said.

"It is not that simple, my dear," Suten cautioned. "Ma-Nefer is a greedy man: he would want full payment with extra. I cannot see him settling for a partial payment. And until your papers arrive and you are able to practice, you have little foundation on which to offer him any form of collateral. And even then, I fear he might put it so high that you will spend years paying it back."

"But surely my mother's jewels, the door and the wooden furniture would cover most of the debt," Neti contended.

"It is best not to react hastily right now," Suten calmly replied. "I'm still looking into the legalities of the situation, but there is not much in the laws. Your father made provision for some exceptions, and I dare say it gives us some leeway, but I know that you are not partial to anyone, and so does the rest of Thebes. So, he could contest any claim of marriage. And I dare say there are some who would be delighted to see you end up with him."

"Yes I can imagine," Neti deadpanned. "I will have to find some way."

"You could approach him and ask if he is willing to let you buy out of the wedding. Find out if it is just the money he is interested in," Suten reasoned.

"I will try," Neti affirmed, nodding her head once.

"That is the best we could hope for; because the only other option where you would be permitted to step away from this is if he was involved in criminal activities against society."

"He is a trader, I don't think he'll do anything that foolish," Neti replied dourly, giving a slight shake of the head.

"Sometimes it is the meekest of sheep who becomes the most dangerous when threatened," Suten Anu averred.

"Yes, Suten, I understand. But he is a coward: he takes his moods and tempers out on those weaker than him. People fear him for what they think he will do." Neti took a deep breath before continuing, "And he uses that to force his ways onto others."

"You have always been a wise child," Suten Anu returned, nodding his head in approval.

"I had a good teacher," Neti avowed.

"Now, do you have any money to tide you over?" Suten Anu asked as he started rolling up the scroll.

"I have a little; I was going to go to the market tomorrow to buy some goods."

Suten Anu looked at her, acknowledging. "How long do you think it will hold you?"

"A few weeks, at least: it's only me."

"Then I will see what I can do here," Suten said, indicating to the scroll.

Just then, Shabaka entered the office. Neti turned her head to look at him, smiling warmly when he nodded his head in greeting, before turning to look back at Suten, stating, "We are going to see Asim."

"You wish to see your parents' bodies again?" Suten asked, his confusion evident in his voice.

"No," Neti quickly replied. "My mother's one amulet is missing. I am hoping that it is there, otherwise it was taken."

"Ah, yes, I understand," Suten said in agreement before turning to look at Shabaka.

"Shabaka has some questions for Asim," Neti quickly added.

"Well then, let me not detain you." Nodding at Shabaka, Suten said, "You are welcome here any time, Shabaka. A friend of Neti's is a friend of mine," the elderly man concluded.

They stepped from Suten's office, turning up the road towards Asim's house. The sun was already baking the mud brick houses, the heat steadily rising as they continued along the road.

"So, did he have any good news for you?" Shabaka spoke once they had advanced some distance from Suten Anu's office.

"Unless Ma-Nefer is doing something illegal, my options are limited. I will go to him later today, and ask him if he would let me buy my way out of the agreement."

"I never knew how rude some of the citizens of Thebes are," Shabaka said as a woman spat in their direction, glaring at them as they passed.

"You get used to it after a while," Neti deadpanned as they moved along the road, some of the people muttering as they passed.

"Yet you don't have a problem with it," Shabaka disbelievingly returned.

"They know no better. My mother always said that people fear things that are different from them."

"It does not excuse bad manners," Shabaka insisted.

Neti looked at him, smiling warmly before replying, "That is also true," inclining her head in acknowledgement. "This way. It is not long until we reach Asim's house, although he will possibly be at the Per-Nefer processing bodies."

"Maybe we should we go there first?" Shabaka questioned, causing Neti to slow down.

"I thought you wished to speak to his wife?" Neti questioned, as she came to a halt before a doorway.

"I do," Shabaka replied, as Neti turned to call, "Tei-ka, are you home?"

A few moments later, an elderly woman appeared in the doorway, her face lighting up when she saw Neti. "Neti, child, what a surprise. Come, come in, please," the woman invited, gesturing with her hand, stepping to one side, and holding the fabric aside for them to enter.

Neti stepped into the room with Shabaka following closely behind, before halting in the main living area.

"Would you like some tea, dear? I was just about to make some."

"That would be lovely," Neti answered.

"This way then," Tei-Ka said indicating to the stairs and leading them up toward the kitchen. "Please sit," Tei-ka invited, pointing to the chairs. "I will move the water to boil."

Neti sat down in one of the chairs, and Shabaka followed suit. Both watching as the elderly lady moved to the stove, before returning to their company, asking, "How are you, my dear? Asim told me about your parents' will. It is difficult to accept something like that."

Neti simply nodded her head in reply before lowering her gaze. "Yes it is. Shabaka has a few questions for you, if you don't mind," she demurely replied.

"Certainly," the woman answered, turning her attention towards the Nubian prefect.

"On the night of Neti's parents' murders, was your husband home?" Shabaka asked, watching as the woman tilted her head slightly.

"He is at home every night: he comes home for dinner and then often returns to his work," she bluntly replied.

Shabaka acknowledged this, then asked, "But two nights ago, was he home for dinner?"

Tei-Ka thought it over for a moment before replying, "He was late, which is nothing unusual. He enjoys going down to the beer house on hot nights," and then she looked at Neti, "No wait! That night he was quite upset about something. But he did not want to talk about it," she added looking at Shabaka.

"Did he have any blood on his clothes?" Shabaka asked, outright.

"Blood? No. Neti will know that they wear different clothes when processing a body. Any blood will land on that. No, he came home in the same clothes he left that morning – stinking of the dead as he usually does on arriving home. I generally have to send him down to the river to wash." The woman started rambling. Neti simply smiled indulgently at her.

"Where is your husband now?"

"He had business to tend to; with the extra work he has needed to see to supplies."

Shabaka nodded his head, "I see. When will he be back then?"

"Soon enough I would think," the woman answered, before turning her attention back to the stove. "Please excuse me, I need to check on the water."

"You think he did it?" Neti interrogated him in hushed tones.

"I'm not certain," Shabaka replied just as lowly, before adding, "she said he had no blood on him. Whoever did that would have been covered in blood. Also had he washed, he would not have reeked of the dead," Shabaka reasoned, before adding, "I will need to have a look at these clothes you wear when working."

"You can come with me when I go to pack up my father's tools," Neti replied.

Tei-ka returned with the pottery cups, handing each of them a cup before taking her seat once again. Just then, a shuffling was heard from the stairs, and Asim appeared at the kitchen. Everyone turned to look at him, before his wife spoke up. "Asim, Neti and her friend are here to see you."

Asim halted dead in his tracks, looking at them in surprise, his body tightening in response before he turned and bolted down the slight stairwell.

"Asim, stop!" Shabaka called after him, quickly placing his cup on the floor, before leaping up in pursuit of the man.

"Asim!" Tei-ka exclaimed in distress, also leaping up from her seat, dislodging the scarf she had around her neck bearing the amulet she wore.

Neti leapt up from her seat, grabbing the woman by her arm and pointing with her free hand towards the amulet, demanding, "Where did you get that?"

"This?" Tia-ka asked gesturing to the amulet. "Asim gave it to me."

"It looks much like my mother's one which is missing," Neti heatedly returned, before demanding, "when did he give it to you?"

"Six, maybe seven nights ago," Tia-Ki answered, uncertainly, nervously adding, "he said it was for good luck. I did not think much of it, but he insists that I wear it. It is pretty, but I do not think it is worth much."

"It is known as a purity of heart amulet," Neti replied letting go of the woman's hand.

Tia-Ki looked at the amulet. "I remember your mother wearing a similar one at times."

"It was her favorite," Neti replied, inclining her head.

"It is missing?" the woman asked, placing a hand on Neti's upper arm.

"I'm not certain," Neti replied.

The old woman acknowledged, before replying, "Come, I guess I shall have to go see about Asim. The old fool will only get himself hurt trying to outrun a prefect."

"Shabaka will not harm him," Neti reassured her, "but why did he run? We mean him no harm."

The elderly woman shook her head. "You know men when they get older: they imagine things. And I think for those who work with the dead, it is worse."

"Why?" Neti asked, never having remembered her father doing anything remotely strange.

"Asim has been very agitated since your parents' deaths. He trusts no one and does not want me leaving the house. I'm not even allowed to talk to strangers."

"It is understandable. Everyone is wary. Shabaka mentioned to me that they will probably be closing the gates of the city."

"I find it hard to believe that that greedy mayor would contest such a thing," Tia-Ki snorted, before asking, "why are you here? You do not think Asim killed your parents?"

"No, I wanted to ask him about my mother's amulet, if it was not still on her body. Also, that if it was, I would like for her to be buried with it."

"He has just finished packing their bodies and was quite upset about it. He said it is wrong to have a body without a heart."

Just then, Shabaka came up the stairs, panting hard. "I lost him. He managed to get away in the parts of town I don't know well. I did not realize embalmers were so fit." He spoke between gasps.

"It is hard work moving bodies around: the work is very physical," Neti returned.

"Madam, where would your husband go?" Shabaka asked having regained his breath.

"I'm not sure: he has many friends."

"I see," Shabaka replied. Turning his attention to Neti, he said, "Come Neti, we should be going."

Tea-Ki turned towards Neti, before speaking. "Neti you are welcome to visit whenever you like. You do not need an invitation: you are like our own daughter."

"Thank you, Tei-ka," Neti sincerely replied. "I will remember."

"Anywhere I could escort you to?" Shabaka asked as they stepped from Asim's home.

"I must go see Ma-Nefer. You could walk with me to his place of business," Neti replied smiling at him.

"I will gladly walk you there."

They arrived at Ma-Nefer's trading post a short while later, and Neti raised her hand to Thoth in greeting as they passed him. Some of the other slaves were moving wares, and simply lowered their gazes when she stepped past them.

Ma-Nefer was sitting on a stool, overseeing his staff with his whip in hand.

Shabaka reached toward Neti, grasping her arm to halt her just outside the striking range of the whip. His familiarity caused her to turn and look at him: noticing his wordless indication of the whip, and inclining her head in understanding.

"I do not want to see you hurt, and he is cruel enough to call it an accident," he quietly murmured.

"What do you want?" Ma-Nefer demanded, looking at the couple before him.

"I came to discuss some business," Neti firmly spoke up.

Ma-Nefer looked over the two of them, before stating, "He is not welcome here. I will not have Nubian slaves sitting in on business; not that a woman can discuss business," he snorted in disbelief. Then looking around, he boomed, "Well get out of here: you know the rules!" Everyone scampered from the room. "You too," he said pointing a finger at Shabaka.

"Neti?" Shabaka questioned in concern.

"I'll be fine Shabaka: you can go," she calmly replied.

"Well you heard the woman: get going," Ma-Nefer sneered.

Shabaka looked at Ma-Nefer, before returning his gaze to Neti. "You know where to find me if you need me."

Neti nodded her head in reply. And with that Shabaka left.

"So what is this business you wish to discuss?" Ma-Nefer pejoratively demanded.

"I would like to buy myself out of our marriage," Neti firmly spoke up.

Ma-Nefer just looked at her in disbelief, before sarcastically replying, "Oh you do? And how do you propose that?"

"There is an amount of wooden furniture in my home, along with the door and my mother's jewels. If you would accept these as a payment toward my father's debts, I will make further payment once I have my papers," Neti replied, standing her ground.

Ma-Nefer simply shook his head, snorting at her. "And you think that would be enough!" he callously replied. "You women are so stupid." Getting up from his seat and moving over to her, he decreed, "And you are the most foolish of them all, claiming to be educated by that old fool. But let me tell you this: when we get married, everything that belongs to you becomes mine. So you are trying to buy yourself out of a marriage with my property."

"It is not yours yet, and I have not consented to a marriage," Neti firmly replied.

Ma-Nefer lifted his hand and struck Neti, her head snapping back before she stumbled and fell to the ground.

"The first thing you will learn is that you are never to speak back to me. You are nothing more than a slave. And I own you," he professed, glaring down at her.

Neti lifted her palm to her face pressing against the throbbing skin of her cheek, her eyes narrowing, as she shook her head.

"I will enjoy whipping you into shape like I did with that useless brother of yours," the man cruelly professed.

"I do not have a brother," Neti heatedly returned.

Just then, Ma-Nefer lifted his whip and swung it, striking her over her one arm and back. Neti cried out in agony as it cracked across her flesh. "Oh yes you have. That sorry excuse of a slave boy out there," Ma-Nefer said pointing in the direction of the vegetable garden. "Oh, your parents never told you. Well now there is an interesting turn of events." Ma-Nefer sneered, "You are nothing more than a common slave. Bought as a child from the same trader I bought your brother."

Neti shook her head in response, before exclaiming, "No! You're lying."

"What!" Ma-Nefer exclaimed, lifting the whip once again. Neti braced for the next strike, clenching her jaw as it struck, only moaning slightly. "I do not lie when it comes to slaves. you shall learn the hard way then," Ma -Nefer decreed, before stomping around the room. His gaze for a moment landing on some pottery jars, a wicked smile crossed his face, "You are worth more to me as a wife, and slave, than your father's – sorry – previous owner's debts," he bitingly stated, before turning toward her. "Once the estate is settled, I will claim what is mine, and that includes you, Now get out of here: you have wasted enough of my time already."

Neti fought against the tears, never in her life having been spoken to in such a manner. She regained her feet and made for the doorway, not even halting when Ma-Nefer called after her, laughing, "I'm going to enjoy breaking you!"

She kept her gaze lowered as she passed Thoth, not even greeting him. Then she turned up the road. Ma-Nefer's voice once again boomed behind her, "What are you looking at you useless piece of flesh? Get back to work!"

Thoth looked at Ma-Nefer, his hands tightening their grip on the implement he was holding. The Nubian slave with him continued his work in the vegetable garden, his dark skin glistening from the sweat. "Come Thoth, do your work. He will only whip you."

"He hit her," Thoth angrily replied. "He's not allowed to do that."

"Allowed or not, it's not worth getting your back cut up," the man quietly replied.

Thoth relented and continued his work.

Neti ran straight to Suten Anu, knowing he would be the one most likely to confirm or reject Ma-Nefer's claim.

She hastily entered his office, and came to a standstill as he exclaimed, "Neti! By the gods, child! What has happened to you?" He rose from his seat, hurrying to her side.

"Ma-Nefer," Neti replied, gasping slightly, before looking at the man in bewilderment.

"He has struck you?" the elderly scribe returned in disbelief, studying her face.

Neti nodded her head in reply, and then waved her hands, before speaking, "That is not important now."

"How so?" Suten Anu asked, looking at her, confused.

"He claims that I'm a slave; that I was bought as a child." She started pacing the room, before turning to look at him, and asking, "Am I? You knew my parents; was I just a slave?"

"My dear girl, calm down," Suten Anu soothed. "You cannot be rash."

"Rash! My world is collapsing around me, and for once, I would just like to know the truth," Neti demanded, her hands clasping into fists.

Suten Anu looked at her for a moment before shaking his head and answering, "I don't know."

"What do you mean you don't know?" Neti heatedly demanded.

"I only met your parents when you were already older, before you came to me for schooling," the scribe honestly replied. "I never knew you as an infant."

His answer had Neti draw in a deep breath.

"And even if you were, it does not change anything," the man professed.

"What!" Neti exclaimed, before adding, "It changes everything. I am a slave: I can be bought and sold, bartered like some piece of property."

"Neti-Kerty!" Suten Anu firmly spoke, drawing her attention. "Have your parents ever treated you as a slave?"

Neti immediately shook her head, her heart pounding. Suten had only rarely needed to reprimand her.

"Then you have your answer," the man said. "A person's actions speak of their intentions. Your parents have never been anything but caring."

"That is no answer," Neti maintained, shaking her head.

"Then you should go speak with Tei-ka," Suten mutedly stated. "She and your mother have always been close."

Neti nodded her head at that, drawing in another deep breath, before turning from the room.

"Just remember," Suten Anu spoke up causing her to turn and look at him. "No matter what you find, your heart knows the truth." Neti nodded her head and continued to the doorway.

"Neti!" Suten called, causing her to look at him again. He reached up to indicate her wig. She righted it before giving him a small smile and leaving.

She arrived at Asim's house not long after, and Tei-ka looked at her in shock, then gestured towards her cheek. "Neti, child, what has happened?"

"Ma-Nefer," Neti responded, giving a slight shrug of the shoulders.

"Come in child. Come to the kitchen: I'll make a herb pack for that," the woman said waving her into the house, leading the way to the kitchen up the small flight of stairs.

"Tei-ka," Neti softly spoke up, "You knew my parents for a long time."

"Yes," the woman said turning her head to glance over her shoulder. "Why do you ask?"

"I heard today that I was bought as a slave," Neti said with a sigh.

The woman turned to her as they entered the kitchen, demanding, "And just where did you hear such a thing?"

"Ma-Nefer," Neti murmured.

"That man should know better to keep his nose in his own matters," the woman professed, making for the storage area.

"It's true, isn't it?" Neti asked, watching the woman's movements.

Tei-ka remained silent for some time, busying herself with preparing the pack, then placing it inside a pot with warm water, before pulling it and coming over to where Neti stood, handing it to her.

Neti looked at the woman as she took it, stating, "You have not answered."

"Sit down." Tei-ka motioned towards the grass mat.

"It is true, isn't it?" Neti insisted, lifting the herb pack to her still throbbing cheek.

"Yes," Tea-Ki hesitantly replied, nodding her head faintly.

"By the gods: I have been a slave all these years!" Neti exclaimed, shaking her head.

"No! Never!" Tea-Ki replied, reaching out to touch Neti's arm. "Please sit, and I will tell you the whole story."

Neti nodded and sat down, looking at the woman as she also took a seat.

Tei-ka looked into the distance for a while, as if trying to remember things, before she began. "You were brought to Thebes along with a big group of slaves," she looked toward Neti and smiling slightly, continued, "you could not even walk properly at that time, so you would not remember it. You were all part of a group of captives that were taken when the pharaoh's men conquered a kingdom. I cannot even remember which one it was, possibly the Hittites – it is not important," the elderly woman dismissed. "Your mother, my dear friend, was barren. They had tried for years to have a child but her womb remained empty. It was also not long after my son had been taken from me by the fever. Your father was looking for a slave to help him in the Per-Nefer. He had saved money for many years, wanting to grow his business. So he and your mother went to the slave market held by the pharaoh: who needed the money for his new city. Your parents always did everything together: things were always well discussed…" The old woman trailed off for a moment, before again starting, "Slave markets are nasty places. But your mother insisted on going with him. And your father was so consumed with love for her that he did not deny her. You were placed in a pen with a bunch of other children, like you were sheep. Many of you were crying…"

"You were there?" Neti asked.

"No, your mother told me. I will never forget the afternoon she walked into our house holding you. She was so happy."

Neti fought against the tears.

"Anyway, the children were kept in this pen, many of them crying, and to your mother it seemed too much. Her heart longing for a child could not cope with their treatment. Most of them were already clothed, all but you." The woman halted for a moment, swallowing before continuing. "You clung to a boy and an older girl. Everyone around your mother was talking about the other children, but none seemed interested in you. And when the older girl was sold: you started wailing. Your mother said it about broke her heart."

"Your father, bless him, had watched her, and approached the merchant, asking about you. The man must have seen your father coming, because he made your father pay the same for you as a male slave," the woman said shaking her head.

"Your mother was so taken by you. She said she had never been happier than the moment you were placed in her arms. You were dirty, with hair everywhere, but to her you were the most beautiful child ever to walk this earth. It was only when they left, that the little boy called out to you, and they realized he was your brother. Your father did not have enough to buy him as well, so your parents came here, and told us about it. I was still hurting from the loss of my son; but Asim said he would make up the deficit and then they could buy the boy together. However, by the time they got back to the market, your brother had already been sold to Ma-Nefer who wanted twice the purchase price for him. We did not have it, and could not raise it. And not long after that Ma-Nefer left for Northern Egypt, on business."

"That is why he has that funny accent," Neti spoke up.

"Yes, Ma-Nefer is originally from Northern Egypt. It was only some seasons later that he returned and settled here."

"Bringing Thoth with him."

"Yes. Your mother recognized the boy; and Ma-Nefer then placed his price at three times that of his purchase, and your parents could not afford it. Then when you started to play together, your parents allowed it. Most would not have permitted their daughter to play with a slave, but your mother did not want to take your brother from you again," the woman concluded.

"But why did they never tell me?" Neti demanded.

"To them, you were their daughter: there was nothing they wouldn't do. You were so eager to learn from both of them, and then from Suten Anu. You were stronger than the other girls: you could stand up for yourself. I think your mother was afraid you would be angry with them, that you would leave and seek out your real family."

"But then why leave me to Ma-Nefer. Why agree?"

"I don't know that. But I know they would not have done it if there had been any other way," the woman returned before pointing at the herb pack that Neti held to her cheek. "Come take that away now: the herbs will have cooled," Tei-ka said, before taking it from her and looking at the area. "Ah, yes, it looks better already," she said before settling again, adding, "you always were their little girl. Her face beamed the first time you called her mamma. She hardly let you out of her sight those first few months. Many thought your father was crazy for buying a girl child. Yet you filled so many hearts: your mother shared you with so many. The joy that filled her heart was there for everyone to see, and that is why your father did what he did."

Chapter 3

Hidden within a darkened alcove of two homes, a pair of eyes watched the beer house across the dusty road. The music and singing within had lessened down some in the last few moments, and he knew it would not be long before the patrons would start leaving: and he would along with them.

It had taken him a few days to find the mason: the one that was interfering. He needed to remove him, to ensure that things went according to plan; nothing could stop him from becoming that what he coveted most.

He glanced up at the stars, gave a faint smile: the gods would be completing the Duat Journey through the underworld. One day he too would undertake that journey with Seth and Horus: as Pharaoh of Egypt. He too would travel the skies with the Sun God Ra, and rule over Egypt: better than Ramesses II ever could. He would be all powerful, a god and a ruler. The one that guided him would show him which hearts he needed to take: hearts that were untarnished by evil deeds. Then he would travel the journey on the Sun Bark, whist the others worked in the fields of reeds.

He gazed at the three-quarter moon. Its light suffused the city with a gray luminosity, allowing its inhabitants free movement: unhindered by the need of lamps and torches. It however made it difficult for him to remain hidden from view. His dark clothes alone caused suspicion in those he had passed earlier. Most citizens revered their white covers, it signified their status, for only the wealthy could afford to wear pure white cotton. But he liked his dark clothes, they allowed him to blend into the shadows. He had to look after this set, as he had needed to do away with the last set, as they had been covered in blood, which had dried before he could rinse them out. This time he was better prepared, it would not be rushed like the last time, this time it was late at night, not around meal times, when others would come visiting.

Children had long since stopped playing on the rooftops. Board games and discussions had also ended as meals were consumed and events discussed. Most of the city's inhabitants would have gone to bed already. The smell of frying meats and freshly baked bread, having long since been replaced by the slightly scented breeze that blew over the Nile: the water having cooled the eastern zephyr as it came into the city.

It was only the younger unattached workers, and those who had a day to themselves, who could afford to socialize until late in the evening.

His attention was momentarily drawn to the doorway of the beerhouse, watching as some of the patrons emerged from within. He scrutinized them as they passed close by him: however none of them were the one he had come for.

 Releasing an agitated sigh, he relented to his wait: unlike the last time, where his actions had been governed by chance. After having waited days for the most opportune moment, he had needed to strike the moment the opportunity had presented itself. He had needed for her to leave the home, with both the old embalmer and his wife remaining... because he could not strike with her present: she had too important a part in the overall plan. She was the one that would assure him his position with the gods.

That evening, with the Nubian prefect once again summonsing her, had offered the perfect opportunity. The old embalmer and his wife had left their door unbarred, in obvious anticipation of her return. It made accessing their home much easier than he had anticipated.

They had already been in their sleeping chamber, something that would have been strange, given the time of day, had it not been for the slight musky scent that had lingered in the air: the couple obviously having taken advantage of their daughter's absence, to fulfill more rudimentary needs. He had captured the old embalmer just as he was about to leave the room, remembering the man's surprise at his presence. He had not had much time: even with her away he needed to speed things along, uncertain as to how long she would be detained: a situation that had not sat well with him. He enjoyed taking his time to watch as the blood flowed from their bodies. To revel in the sensations that filled him as their life force drained from them. He had quickly moved to knock them out, returning them to their bed, before setting to work. There had been no time for finesse, they were to be his first, and he had to hurry and get out of the house before she returned.

He had hacked at the chests, pulling out their still beating hearts: the blood had run down his arms, its hot stickiness sent tingles through his skin. It filled him with vigor. It made him powerful: he could take a life. He could decide when it was time for them to die… he was truly a god: for only gods could do such things.

Movement from the beerhouse doorway once again drew his attention. He watched as the mason appeared from the doorway: obviously inebriated.

"Sinuhe, are you going to be okay to walk home on your own?" one of his friends asked, when they too appeared from the doorway.

"Yes, I'll be fine," the mason started, staggering slightly. "There's a good moon, it's a short walk," he said righting himself, before loudly declaring, "the worst that can happen is I can walk into that old woman that wanders the streets."

The others laughed at that, the one even declaring, "Well she'd take care of you, not that you'd be much use to her," before taking their leave in the opposite direction.

He remained within the darkened alcove, watching as they left, repeatedly gripping the heavy wooden handle he held: he had picked it up at the refuse site a while back, and had accustomed himself with its weight.

He waited for the mason to move away from the beerhouse, and then followed him. The young man staggered slightly and regained himself, before looking about him.

One of the street cats scurried along the streets and hissed at him as he passed it, causing the young mason to turn around and look in his direction. He halted, once again blending in with the shadows surrounding him, watching – waiting.

"Anyone back there?" the young mason asked, peering into the distance, swaying slightly on his feet, before turning to continue up the road.

Careful to remain hidden in the shadows, he followed. Watching as the young man from time to time looked over his shoulder, his pace increasing slightly.

The mason finally disappeared into one of the worker's homes, and he waited in the shadows for a while: allowing the man to find his way about his home. From the sound of things he was staggering about, alarmingly.

He smiled: it would be easy to take the man's heart, and waited until the only sounds he could hear were those of his own pounding heart, the crickets chirping at night and a mouse scurrying about close by.

His heart was thumping in anticipation of what was to come. He felt that strange sensation once again overcome him, the one that made him feel capable of anything, as he prepared to enter the mason's home. He pushed aside the cloth covering the doorway before stepping inside, and gave his eyes a moment to adjust to the darkness that filled the room. The faint light filtering in from the high windows allowed him to carefully navigate the home without disrupting anything, and not long after his entry, he reached the mason's bedchamber. He moved the fabric covering the door out of the way: only to discover that the man was already lying face down on the bed, possibly passed out from too much beer.

He approached the bed, almost stumbling over the small grass mat covering the floor, when the man mumbled something and moved slightly on the bed. He lifted the heavy handle, aiming for the best area, then brought it firmly down, knocking the man hard behind the head.

The blow, he knew, was powerful enough to knock the man out completely, but not kill him. Dropping the heavy handle next to the bed, he moved closer to assess the man, grabbing his shoulder to turn him over. His hand immediately moved to the man's chest, feeling for his heartbeat below the breastbone. A smile tugged at his lips as he felt the organ's thumping.

An excited giggle escaped his lips at the anticipation, the thought of blood flowing freely, the thought spurring him into action as he reached back for his flint knife that was safely secured below his dark robe. His heart raced, as his mind cast off anything but the task at hand. His eyes remained fixed to the man's chest and as he brought the knife closer to it a tingling sensation took over his body.

He could take his time on this occasion: and he was going to enjoy it. He felt along the breastbone, until it came to an end, then carefully cut into the skin just below the ribs: he must not damage the heart, for it would mean nothing then. It was also too difficult to break the bones around the chest: it took too much time. He watched as the blood flowed from the cut: the dark trail progressed along the skin, dripping down onto the bed linen, pooling slightly, before being absorbed into the fabric.

He captured some of it on his fingertips and lifted it to his mouth, tasting the warm sticky liquid, the slight metallic aftertaste remaining on his tongue. A giddy sense of euphoria took hold. The letting of blood was considered by some healers to be medicinal: he could feel the power enter him; he was becoming a god, with godly powers.

Drunk on power he made the cut deeper, cutting through the skin: the cut a few times longer than his hand. He reached into the opening, the warm sticky blood covering his hands, as he broke the membrane under the ribs. He could feel the tissue push against his hand as he forced his way up between the lungs. His fingers stoked against the man's still beating heart. A wave of ecstasy rushed over his body, causing him to become aroused.

He wanted to see it, wanted to watch it beat in the man's chest. He pulled his hand out reaching once again for the knife as he slashed at the chest, the blood flowing freely. With a giddy giggle, he pulled the skin away from the bone. Excited grunts came from him as he started breaking the bones. He pulled at the bones, drawing them aside: but it was too dark in the room for him to see. His one hand reached down to stroke himself, it was good, so good.

He reached into the cavity once again, his hand wrapping around the mason's still beating heart; as his body released, he grunted his pleasure sitting back slightly, his mind glazed in its euphoric state.

His fingers once again closed around the heart, taking hold of it. He pulled it back, feeling it thump faster in his hand. He severed the first artery, giggling when the heart sped up some more sending blood all over the mason's chest and sheets. He severed the other vein, lifting the beating heart from the body, quickly severing the last two before lifting the still beating heart up over his head: offering it to the gods. The remaining blood squirted from it and ran down his arms, some of it falling on his face. He stuck his tongue out, licking off the drops that fell on his lips, reveling in the taste of his deed.

"It's mine now," he chortled, as the heart started failing, "soon I will be one of you!" he announced, sniggering slightly, before looking down at the dead body before him.

The heart in his hand stopped beating, and a wave of sensation bubbled up his spine. His entire body felt energized, as the sensations took hold.

He reached underneath his once-again blood-soaked clothes for the cloth he had brought with him. Pulling it out, he lay it on the bed before wrapping the heart in it and moving from his position. His feet landed in a pool of blood as he rose from the bed, causing him to smile smugly with satisfaction. He bent to retrieve his handle, before turning and moving from the body, leaving a trail of bloody prints as he let himself out of the house.

He glanced up the road, knowing he could not be seen in his current state: the blood already becoming sticky, with some of it setting on his skin. He once again faded into the shadows, making his way back to the passage that led to the hidden chamber: where he would process the heart, in order to keep its spirit intact.

Entering the chamber, he walked toward the platform, placing the heart on it, before turning to collect the decorated canoptic jar he had prepared for it. He placed it on the platform and collected the palm wine and extra natron, placing them next to an earthenware bowl.

He opened the cloth to reveal the heart and lifted it away from the material. He washed the heart with palm wine before placing it in the canoptic jar already half filled with natron; then carefully added more of the salt, before closing the lid.

He checked the jar to make certain there was no blood on the outside before gathering up the equipment, leaving the heart there.

He cleaned and packed away all of the equipment, before going to see to his clothes: he could not return to his sleeping chamber covered in blood.

Stepping outside the chamber, he stripped off his clothes, then drew water from the pail he had set there earlier, and set about cleaning himself. Only a few more hearts, a few more nights like tonight and I will be energized: I too will be a god.

Shabaka approached the mingling crowd in the road: the young runner having reported the death had warned him of the hostility within the gathering crowd. Their low agitated mumbling could be heard several yards away, with their petulance visible even at a distance.

When the pharaoh had assigned him to Thebes, he had not thought he would need to deal with as many hostile situations. His orders had seemed so simple: discover the source of the discrepancies and to report his findings to the Palace. However, his time since arriving in the city had been spent looking at dead bodies and inspecting suspect circumstances, rather than making any headway on the actual reason for his appointment there. A matter that was frustrating him to no end, never having thought he would remain in the city for longer than half a season.

Most of the city's citizens had chosen to remain aloof, which had been welcoming at first. However, he soon realized that they did not embrace strangers: especially those who held a position of authority and originating from their concurred territories. Though, he could not carp about the season he had already spent there. The guards and officers under him were all respectful, working well as a team; and he had also met Neti.

A smile crossed his face at the thought of her name, and how they had met. How he had almost chased her from the room that day, intent on reprimanding the guard for allowing her entry...

It had been half a moon phase after his appointment in Thebes, when one of the runners had summonsed him to examine another body: an elderly man, the fourth death he had dealt with since his arrival. The man's friend had found him on the main room floor of his house, and had notified the guard.

Shabaka had still been familiarizing himself with the officers and the city at the time, and everyone had been standing around, mumbling to each other: speculating that the man had obviously died from some problem with his body, when she had arrived.

Her entry had drawn everyone's attention. She was strikingly attractive, entering the room with poise and purpose. It had been her confidence, her self-possessed presence that had drawn him most: rendering him monetarily dumbfounded.

She had looked about the room, nodding her head in greeting at the one officer, before making for the body: a rolled up scroll in her hand. He had been about to reprimand her, when two bearers had joined her, turning over the body so that she could inspect it. She had knelt next to the body, tilting her head slightly as she looked at it. Moments later she had commented about the man having died in that position, and that his blood-filled eyes confirmed that it had been something to do with his breathing. Her comment had drawn him closer to her, wanting to ask how she knew that, when she had simply risen from her position and instructed the two bearers to take the body. The men had immediately complied, whilst she turned toward the officer in charge, extending the papyrus scroll to him. The officer had in turn indicated toward him, and she had simply turned to look his way. She inclined her head in greeting and extended the papyrus scroll for him to take. Then she turned and followed the bearers out of the room.

It was only later that he discovered her name, and that she was an embalmer's daughter, who often came with the bearers to collect the bodies her father was to process. He had sought her out, fascinated by her comments about the body, and had quickly discovered the whereabouts of her father's Per-Nefer.

She had welcomed him one day; and had shown him the body they were preparing; explaining to him what had caused the man's death, showing him various markings on the body. Her knowledge of the human body had been astounding, and unlike many women, she had been unperturbed in the presence of bodies.

With time, he requested her input more frequently: it often helped him to distinguish if a death was due to murder, or bodily problems. And with the recent escalation of murders, he had come to depend on her input to establish if any of them needed any further inquest.

However, with the recent loss of her parents, he had been uncertain on whether or not he should call upon her services with the newest incident. He had sent the young runner on to beckon her, hoping she would be willing to help him once more, he would understand if she declined. The murder of her parents haunted him, the scene, the blood: it had been so violent, so unnecessary. He could only imagine how she felt... he only hoped that their deaths had nothing to do with his presence there, and the actual reason of his assignment.

He hoped that their murder had nothing to do with his presence, or her assistance with it.

"I tell you it was that witch, she did it!" an angry retort broke his train of thought, causing him to look out over the crowd

"I told Sinuhe something was going happen to him, that he shouldn't have spoken to her," another loudly professed, causing Shabaka to focus on two younger men within the crowd.

He walked over to them, before asking, "You knew the man?" whilst indicating towards the guarded doorway.

"Yes, Sinuhe worked with us. I told him he was a fool for talking to her, even bigger for helping her," the second man professed.

Shabaka looked them over, noting their physique and work hardened hands.

"This is her handiwork. I tell you," the first one avowed.

Shabaka felt his brow furrow, "Who's?" he asked, for a moment confused.

"That witch of the dead, only she would do something like this," the second man decreed. This caused Shabaka to look pointedly at them, before asking, "What does Neti-Kerty have to do with this?" It still confused him as to why they referred to her as such.

"She came looking for mud, and he stupidly enough gave her some," the first man said, "and that's why he's dead."

"There is no reason why anyone would want him dead," the second man spoke up. "He was well liked by all of us."

"I'll come speak to you again," Shabaka said before taking his leave of the two men, and moving towards the guarded doorway.

The guard pulled the fabric door cover aside, and Shabaka bowed slightly to enter the home. The coppery scent permeating the air, had him slow his movement slightly, swallowing as he steeled himself for what he anticipated finding within the other room. For a moment, he questioned whether it had been such a good idea to have Neti summonsed before he himself had even seen the body.

He stepped into the mason's private room, and was once again greeted by a bloody sight. The walls were covered in blood, with the man's chest violently ripped open: his heart also missing. Once again, there was a trail of bloody footprints leading from the room and Shabaka knew, without a doubt, that whoever the killer was, they would be looking for the same man that killed Neti's parents.

Shabaka walked to the side of the bed, noticing the young man's features, and wondered about the man's interaction with Neti. If it could in any way have led to his death, and if so, how?

"For the love of Horus! What is this?" the familiar booming voice of Thebes's mayor filled the room, causing Shabaka to take a deep breath, before clenching his jaw tightly in order to prevent himself from retorting to the mayor that it was a murder scene, and they had work to do. He however righted himself and turned towards the mayor, before calmly stating, "Morning, Mayor. Anything I can help you with?"

"No, I just came to see what all the commotion was about," the mayor apathetically replied, shifting slightly on his feet and looking past Shabaka toward the body. He appeared unwilling to step further into the room, and remained in the doorway, his hands wringing slightly.

"There's nothing much to see," Shabaka pronounced, and he looked about the sparsely furnished room, before returning his gaze to the mayor and flatly stating, "the man did not own much. So, there will not be much to tax him on either. There is no reason for your presence here."

"And you think that that is why I am here?" the mayor once again boomed, "that all I worry about is the taxes these people pay?"

"No, actually I don't know why you are here; just that you seem to show up at every incident, interfering with the inquiry of each," Shabaka decreed, looking directly at the man.

"I am the mayor of this town!" Pa-Nasi angrily exclaimed, before concluding, "Need I remind you of that fact."

"No, I am well aware of that," Shabaka calmly replied, "but like you, I was also appointed by the pharaoh, to deal with these situations," he added, indicating to the body.

"You may deal with such situations," the mayor impertinently started, before defiantly asserting, "but I am still the one who decides whether the body receives a funded entombment."

"The man is a young mason," Shabaka started in disbelief, "what possible contribution has he made to the city to warrant the use of tax money for his burial?"

"That, is for me to decide," the mayor arrogantly stated.

Just then a tall man, with a scar slanting over his one eye, entered the room, and Shabaka looked the man over, for a moment wondering about the man's crimes: the mark on his face being similar to those of the Kenbet. However, Shabaka did not contemplate this for long, as the newcomer was soon flanked by two sturdier men.

The man looked at Shabaka for a while, before pointing to the corpse. "I've come to collect the body."

Shabaka looked the man over again and gave a slight shake of the head. Unable to recall his face, he firmly demanded, "And you are?"

"Karndesh, I am an embalmer," the man calmly stated, before looking at the men flanking him, indicating as he spoke up, "These are my bearers."

"Then why have I not met you before?" Shabaka was quick to ask.

"I am entrusted with the civil funded funerals. I have been tasked with cleaning this body for burial," the man said, nodding towards the bloody body on the bed.

Shabaka looked towards the mayor for a moment, before turning his attention to the man, "I would like Neti-Kerty to have a look at the body first."

"Ha! That witch, I don't think those outside would even allow her close to the body," the mayor derisively started, "and what could she possibly tell you that you cannot see for yourself," he continued, glancing towards the body. "Clearly the man's heart was ripped from his chest. I do not know why you insist on her seeing the body. She cannot possibly help you find who did this by looking at the body. She is nothing but a wrongly educated woman," the mayor concluded, before turning to Karndesh and ordering him, "take the body, you do not need to heed his wishes."

Shabaka stepped towards the mayor, before intrepidly challenging, "Should I report back to the Vizier that you are impeding on my duties. I do not think the pharaoh would appreciate such news from Thebes."

The mayor pulled himself up to his full height, before averring, "There is nothing that woman can do for him. I tend to agree with the crowd out there that she could have done it."

"That is not physically possible," Shabaka boldly decreed. "Neti is not strong enough to have fought off a mason, so how could she have killed …" Shabaka trailed off as the crowd outside started up in a roar, drawing his attention away from their conversation.

The guard outside the fabric door stepped inside, anxiously glancing about the room until his gaze came to reset on Shabaka. "Prefect," he addressed Shabaka, "you had better come see this."

Shabaka stepped past the mayor and out of the mason's room, moving stealthily to the main doorway. Pushing the fabric aside, he stepped out into the bright daylight: his heart immediately racing when he saw the crowd gathered around Neti, calling her names and shoving her between them. "Stone her! She is one of Apopis's servants," a woman within the crowd called. "Burn her body, condemn her to her god's side," another piped, "she is evil."

"What is going on here?" Shabaka demanded harshly, causing everyone to stop and look at him. "Let her go!" he commanded, looking pointedly at the one man who held her in his grasp. The man shoved her towards the ground, causing her to stumble and land on her knees. "Now back off," Shabaka commanded, "if anyone so much as harasses her, I will have them brought before the Kenbet," Shabaka decreed as Neti rose to her feet. Her wig was slightly askew, as she dusted off her hands and looked down at her slip, noticeably rattled.

"She is not welcome here," the one woman shouted; then spat on the ground.

Neti righted her clothes, and wig, keeping her gaze lowered. Shabaka took hold of her arm drawing her to his side. The action caused her to glance up at him, allowing him to see the tears glistening in her eyes, and how she blinked to prevent them from falling

"That is enough, she has as much right to be here as you," he commanded to those present, "and challenge me on that, and you will be the first to appear before the Kenbet."

The group of people quickly backed off, murmuring amongst themselves.

Just then, the embalmer with the scar exited the door, his two bearers conveying the wrapped body as they walked past them, the mayor in their wake.

"Who is he?" Neti asked in confusion, looking after the departing faction.

"That is what I was hoping you could tell me," Shabaka replied drawing her attention. "He claims to be an embalmer."

Neti turned her head to look at the group before professing, "I've never seen him."

"You know all the embalmers, right?" Shabaka asked, causing her to look at him.

"Yes, we're a close-knit community," Neti replied, nodding her head absentmindedly, "But I've never met him."

Shabaka looked at her for a moment, before asking, "Are you okay?"

Neti looked at him, before giving a slight nod of the head and replying, "Yes, just a little manhandled."

Shabaka looked at her in disbelief, but then indicated down the road, before bidding, "Come, I will walk you home."

"You don't need me then?" Neti asked, confused.

"The mayor has already had the body removed, and I think it is best if maybe you didn't see the room," Shabaka said as they started their return journey.

"Why?" Neti asked, falling into step next to him.

"His heart was taken: so I don't think there is much you would have been able to do."

"Oh," Neti replied, then looked at him, reaching for his arm: effectively halting their progress, "were there any bloody footprints?"

"Yes, there were," Shabaka replied, before looking down to where her hand was resting on his arm; watching as she hastily withdrew it. Her gaze dropped to the ground for a moment, before they continued along the road again.

"Have you heard from Asim?" Shabaka asked a short while later.

"No, why?" Neti replied looking towards him.

"I've had guards posted outside his house, but he hasn't returned home. Tea-Ka hardly moves from the house. Something is not right there."

"I don't think he had anything to do with it," Neti professed.

"I know you're partial to the man, because of his connection to your family, but it looks damning for him," Shabaka candidly replied.

"I need to see the body," Neti suddenly decreed, halting suddenly.

"Why?" Shabaka asked turning to look at her.

"Embalmers have a certain way of cutting a body, very often it is unique to them, to the size of their hands," Neti said, lifting her hand. "My father used to make the initial incision twice that of his hands width: he always said that way he did not harm any of the entrails when he withdrew them."

"You think you could possibly identify who it could be?" Shabaka asked in disbelief.

"No, but I will be able to tell you if an embalmer did it," Neti said.

"By only the cut?"

"Embalmers know how to cut a body to be able to extract the internal organs through only one cut," Neti clarified.

Shabaka looked at her for a moment, before nodding his head and replying, "We can go and have a look, but I first want you to make sure you weren't hurt just now. We will have to track this embalmer down."

"That is easily enough achieved," Neti replied, causing Shabaka to look at her, "all embalmers are listed with the overseer of embalmers, he reports to the overseer of high priests. If this embalmer is practicing in Thebes he would have to be listed."

"Where do we find this overseer?"

"Marlep acts as Thebes's overseer. He oversees the main Per-Nefer. He will know where to find him."

Later that same morning, Pa-Nasi made his way into the beer house. It was mid morning and he was irritated from the morning's interlude with the prefect. The darkened room was cooler than outside, however filled with the familiar scent of fermented grain. The grass mats on the floor were still neatly arranged, it would be some time before the others would arrive for a drink. He greeted the owner in passing, nodding his head when the man indicated to an earthenware cup, then continued further into the room, finally locating Ma-Nefer in the corner they frequented whenever meeting.

Ma-Nefer was already seated with a beer, and looked up as he approached, inclining his head in greeting.

"I have more important matters to attend to than to meet you here for trifling matters," the mayor spoke up.

"And yet you are here," Ma-Nefer arrogantly replied, indicating for the mayor to join him.

Pa-Nasi took one of the seats, glancing about the room, watching as one of the serving women approached them. He looked her over, contemplating if he should discuss a tryst with the owner, but instead took the beer from her and returning his attention to Ma-Nefer, demanded "So what did you want?"

"I need a favour," Ma-Nefer flatly stated, looking pointedly at the man.

The mayor regarded him, lifting both brows before replying, "With?"

"Neti-Kerty," Ma-Nefer replied, frustrated.

The mayor scoffed at that. "Your future wife already causing you some problems? I told you she'd be trouble."

"She's not the problem, I'm actually looking forward to breaking her," Ma-Nefer started, a sly grin forming on his lips. "I need her papers intercepted, she cannot receive them until we are married."

"Why?" The mayor asked taking a sip from his beer, the cool slightly grainy fluid rushing down his throat, soothing the dry sensation that had formed there.

"One of my men told me Suten Anu sent a scroll to the Kenbet this morning," Ma-Nefer started, "I'm not certain that the will is as straightforward as I believed it to be: she has already approached me wanting to buy out of the marriage."

"Not that I blame the woman," Pa-Nasi scoffed. "You're not exactly the Nubian prefect she seems to have taken a fancy to."

"Be that as it may, I have far better use for her skills," Ma-Nefer professed.

"I will see what I can do about her papers," Pa-Nasi returned, once again taking a draw from his beer.

"Now all I need to do is lessen her assets she holds, so that she cannot buy out of the marriage," Ma-Nefer thoughtfully mumbled: more to himself.

"Why don't you get Kadurt to do some documents for you; make some claim against the house that needs to be paid," Pa-Nasi calmly spoke up, causing Ma-Nefer to look at him, then nod his head slightly.

"That is an idea," Ma-Nefer concurred.

The mayor started swirling his beer in his mug, watching it slop around and around, before asking, "When is your next shipment of goods moving out?"

"We're getting ready to leave in two days," Ma-Nefer replied. "Everything is in order."

The mayor lifted his gaze from his cup, and looked pointedly at Ma-Nafer, stressing, "Let's just hope they don't run into trouble, like last time."

"There was no trouble," Ma-Nefer replied, shrugging his shoulders slightly, "It was taken care of."

The mayor released a frustrated sigh, before speaking, "This Shabaka is getting on my nerves, and I would think yours as well. It seems that little wife to be of yours is rather taken by him. They seem to spend a lot of time together lately."

Ma-Nefer simply shrugged his shoulders, "Who knows, maybe she'll distract him enough. He'll leave anyway, when he fails to find what the pharaoh sent him for. And once we're married she's going to make me a wealthy man."

"You've had queries?" the mayor asked in surprise.

"A few of our colleagues, I just need to get her fully isolated from the townspeople."

"Well this morning's little episode should help with that," the mayor stated before taking another draw of his beer.

"Yes I heard," Ma-Nefer replied, nodding his head.

Neti-Kerty and Shabaka ascended the steps leading to Thebes's largest Per-Nefer chambers. The high-roofed building with its impressive pillared entrance, festooned with hieroglyphics honoring the gods, was divided into a series of chambers: where individual embalmers set about their work whilst training up the next generation of embalmers.

Their entrance was greeted by the familiar smell of burning spices: the smell originating from the lamps lighting the main chamber, all being filled with a herd infused oil. The smell, although overwhelming, could not completely dispel the stench of dead bodies.

"I do not recall other Per-Nefers smelling like this," Shabaka commented, slowing his stride slightly.

"Marlep often has to deal with already rotted bodies. The main Per-Nefer is charged with the removal and processing of all bodies. The smaller Per-Nefers have personal clients we are responsible for, which is why they do not smell," Neti explained as she walked towards Marlep.

"Marlep," Neti greeted the embalmer, as she came to stand before him.

Marlep turned to look at her and smiled warmly, before starting, "Well now, if it isn't little Neti-Kerty; what brings you here? Or have you gotten your papers from Anum and need to enlist?"

Neti shook her head, then replied, "No we're looking for a embalmer named…" Neti halted and then turned to look at Shabaka, who added, "Karndesh, he has a scar over his one eye."

Marlep acknowledged, replying, "I know him, he arrived here a few months ago. Holds full papers from Anum. Figured it strange at first that he would select Thebes to practice, but he is a quiet man, keeps to himself."

Shabaka looked at Neti, before asking Marlep, "Do you know where we can find him?"

"Sure," Marlep replied indicating the passage, "he works in the far chamber on the right: handles most of the civil funded funerals. He comes in, does his work and leaves at night. Come I'll take you to him," Marlep invited, starting to move towards the passage.

Neti and Shabaka followed in his wake, Shabaka asking, "Is he busy?"

"Not really," Marlep answered. "He does a few bodies a month, and helps if we're overrun."

"You've checked his work?" Shabaka asked.

"He works neat enough, but receives no supervision. He does civil funerals requiring the minimal preparation of the body. I know he had bearers bring in another body this morning, so he might be busy at the moment," Marlep replied, as they came to a halt outside a heavy drape.

"That is why we want to see him. I want Neti to have a look at the body,"

Marlep looked at Neti for a moment, before stating, "You do realize that the body was also cut open like your parents?"

Neti nodded her head, before replying, "Yes, I was warned."

Marlep drew the heavy drapes aside, allowing them access to the chamber. Their entry had Karndesh turn to look at them, before suddenly throwing his hands up, exclaiming, "No-no-no no, no women are allowed in here."

"Easy Karndesh, Neti is one of us," Marlep professed.

Neti's gaze landed on the body lying on the platform, the bandages and the flagon of anointing oil: the room suddenly dimming.

She was a young girl again, her mother having sent her to call her father to dinner. She moved the doorway drapery out of the way, stepping into the chamber. She was not scared of these people her father worked with, they were always quiet. They just lay there whilst he worked on them. Some darker than the others, some of their skins were softer to touch. Her father was rubbing the oil her mother helped him prepare. She often helped with gathering the herds. The man he was working on was being wrapped: she had even helped her father, handing him the bandages and amulets.

"Neti, child, what brings you here?" Her father asked, as he continued to rub oil over the body.

"Mama said to call you for dinner," Neti said stepping closer and looking at the body with its slightly hollowed torso. "I can help," she offered, stepping towards the bandages.

"After dinner," her father said, reaching to pull the sheet over the man's body…

"Neti?" Shabaka's voice called her back to the present, startling her slightly and causing her to look at him questioningly.

"Are you okay?" he asked, touching her shoulder.

Neti nodded her head in response, clearing her throat slightly, a lump having settled within it.

Just then, Karndesh spoke up as pulled the sheet over the body he was working on, "The mayor said I was not to let her anywhere near the body."

Marlep indicated to Shabaka, and spoke up, "Prefect Shabaka was appointed by the pharaoh himself. His authority supersedes that of the mayor's when it comes to these matters."

Karndesh acknowledged this and pointed over to the other platform, where a body lay covered with a sheet. "I have not yet started on him, I need to finish wrapping this one first."

Neti and Shabaka made their way over to the other body, Neti looking around the room, sniffing the air slightly. A frown formed on her brow at an unfamiliar scent.

"Something wrong?" Shabaka reservedly asked.

Neti turned to look at him, tilting her head slightly, before giving him an almost imperceptible nod.

They stopped next to the platform, with Marlep grasping the sheet and drawing it back from the body.

Neti gasped when she saw the face, "By Osiris!" Neti exclaimed, clamping her hand over her mouth and stepping back from the body.

"What is it?" Shabaka asked turning toward her.

Neti pointed at the body, for a moment struggling to breathe. "That is the mason I met the other day, he gave me mud for my parents' bedroom."

Marlep made to cover the body again, but Neti halted him, "No, it's okay." Then she stepped forward to look at the body.

"Are you going to be okay?" Shabaka asked, coming to stand next to her.

Neti nodded her head, before replying. "Just shocked." She looked at the man's chest, inspecting the gashes and their crude manner; then stepping back and drawing Shabaka with her, "I need to have a look at the other body." She, indicated to the body Karndesh was still standing next to.

"Why?" Shabaka asked, confused.

"Something smells wrong, and I think it's that body," Neti professed.

"I thought you wanted to see this body," Shabaka replied, for a moment put out.

"He is the only embalmer I do not know," Neti said mutely, "The gashes in this body were made in anger. Not many know exactly where to find the heart. It also takes a lot of strength to open the chest."

"You think he will let us?" Shabaka asked, glancing toward the scarred embalmer.

"Something is strange: he does not want us here. See how he glances about; people who are nervous of my presence do that. No embalmer has ever feared me," Neti decreed.

"So what do we do?" Shabaka asked in a low voice.

Neti calmly enunciated, "Have Marlep escort him out, you have the authority to order it."

"Okay," Shabaka replied, nodding his head firmly, then turning towards Marlep. "Marlep I would like for you to escort Karndesh from the chamber."

"What! No! You can't do that," the embalmer fiercely retorted.

"And my reason for such action?" Marlep calmly requested.

"Neti wishes to discuss matters pertaining to our inquiry, whilst looking at the body," Shabaka calmly assured.

"Yes it is understandable. Come Karndesh, we shall leave them," Marlep beckoned the embalmer to accompany him.

"But this is my chamber, they have no right to do this," the embalmer protested.

"Shabaka's position means his requests are sanctioned by the pharaoh," Marlep started, "come we will go have some bread and beer whilst they discuss matters." Marlep, gestured for the man to precede him from the room, before pointedly looking over his shoulder at Neti.

Neti nodded her head slightly, before moving closer to the body on the platform. Once they were out of the chamber, she made over to the other body.

"So what are you looking for?" Shabaka asked as Neti lifted the end of the sheet and drew it away from the body.

"Before he covered it, I noticed that something was wrong with the skin's color; and the smell is wrong," Neti said examining the body.

"What do you mean? Do bodies smell differently then?" Shabaka asked looking down at the one before them.

"Yes, each embalmer uses herbs when they prepare a body. Depending on the combinations the smell obtained differs. Some of them are so distinct that one could identify an embalmer by it." Neti, glanced for a moment in the flagon, sniffing its contents. "Cedar oil," she stated aloud, before turning to the body. "See here." She indicated the skin over the ribs and torso, "The skin usually darkens on preservation. It will eventually turn black. This body has not been in natron for long, or at least not long enough for wrapping."

"How do you know he is going to wrap it?" Shabaka asked, looking at the body.

"The presence of cedar oil and bandages tells me that. The body is rubbed down with the oil and wrapped with bandages, and amulets inserted in certain areas."

"You should tell me more about this sometime," Shabaka commented, watching as Neti inspected the corpse's face.

Neti lifted her gaze from the body to look at him, "You should come around for dinner one evening. I'll show you my scrolls," Neti replied before checking the corpse's eyes. "Just as I thought," she proclaimed, turning from the body and moving over to the implements. She selected a curved hook before returning to the body and inserting the end on it into the left nostril. She pushed it up until it stopped; then knocked it hard. A cracking sound emanated from the body, followed by a gagging sound beside her, causing her to turn and look at Shabaka: who had his hand over his mouth. "The first one is always the worst," Neti said, before pulling the hook out and looking at the matter on the end: her nose wrinkling slightly at the smell.

"This body has not been properly prepared," she decreed, turning to show Shabaka the hook. Shabaka in turn just stepped back from her. "He has not taken out the brain and the eyes have not been replaced with resin balls," Neti said placing the hook to the side. She moved to check the mouth, before stating, "It also has not been filled."

Shabaka remained at a distance as he watched her stroke her hand over the body.

"He is still too rounded to be wrapped, there should be slight indentions over the ribs, especially if he had his organs removed." Neti ran her hand over the stomach, suddenly stopping to feel the area, her brow furrowing.

"What is it? Shabaka asked, stepping closer again.

"This is wrong," she stated as she felt the area, then turning to look at Shabaka, "look in those jars there, and see if his intestines are in there," she requested, lifting the hook again and causing Shabaka to visibly shudder. She placed it back in its place, instead picking up the flint knife and turning back to the body.

"There's some stuff in here mixed with a salt," Shabaka replied, holding the one jar askew for her to see.

"He did not even clean them properly before placing them inside," Neti said, shaking her head.

"What are you doing?" Shabaka asked, slightly distraught, as Neti cut away the stitching.

"He's put something in here, and I want to know what it is," Neti stated, as she pulled away the stitching, decreeing, "he should not be so disrespectful of the dead, I'll report him."

Neti parted the skin, opening the cut and pulling the resin bandage away from it, placing it on the side. She reached into the body and extracted a hard lump of cloth from it. "What in Horus's name has he put in here?" Neti asked, opening the piece of fabric: revealing an unpolished emerald. Her heart started racing, as she dropped it in shock, her hand flying to her mouth. "Oh dear Oitis, what is he doing?"

Shabaka bent down to retrieve the gem, looking at it before righting himself, watching as Neti once again reached into the body extracting another wrapped lump: unwrapping it to reveal a lump of amethyst.

"So that's how they are doing it," Shabaka mutely rejoined next to her.

"Who?" Neti asked, turning to look at him in disbelief.

"This is how they're getting the gems out of the city," Shabaka said looking at her, "how many gems are in there do you think?"

"It would take a lot to fill a body of this size, and it feels quite full," Neti replied pushing on the abdomen of the body, then suddenly turning to Shabaka, "you knew of this," Neti firmly decreed, "that is why you are not surprised."

Shabaka nodded his head, "It is the reason the pharaoh appointed me here." Shabaka looked about them for a moment before stepping closer to Neti. "There were discrepancies in the records, between that which was mined, and the gems arriving at the palace. I was tasked with uncovering the dishonesty. Up until today I have not managed to find anything, whoever is behind this is cunning, and resourceful. They have done this for seasons already without being caught, and now I understand how: no one is going to search a body being escorted from town."

"What are we gong to do now, we cannot just leave it like this," Neti replied, indicating to the body.

"Can you close him up?" Shabaka asked.

"The stitching was a bit crude, but yes I could," Neti replied.

"Put these back and close him up," Shabaka said handing her the two gems, "we will make as if we have found nothing. I will have guards monitor the building. I want to know who else is …'

"You're not going to approach Karndesh?" Neti asked, surprised.

"I think he just prepares the body and gems for transport. I want to know how they get these bodies out of the city, and who is bringing the gems to them. I want to capture them all," Shabaka stated before turning to Neti, "thank you."

"What for?" Neti returned surprised.

"For noticing the differences," Shabaka sincerely replied, helping to right the chamber whilst she stitched up the corpse. They replaced the sheet, and glanced about the room one last time: before stepping past the heavy drape and into the passageway.

"So you're certain that the cut was made by someone familiar with bodies?" Shabaka asked as they approached Marlep and Karndesh.

"Yes, the person had to know where the heart was situated to take it out," Neti replied.

"So you are finished?" Karndesh asked, looking from one to the other.

"Yes, we are, Neti here can be very informative," Shabaka said looking sideways at her, "she explained to me how you remove the intestines for preservation."

"Yes, I hope her papers come soon. The loss of her father will be felt. But she is truly capable of filling his shoes," Marlep professed.

Neti and Shabaka left not long after that.

"You think Marlep might be in on it?" Shabaka asked as they moved from the building.

"I'm not sure, he might be. He's always been respectful to me though," Neti honestly replied.

"And Asim?"

"Oh I don't think so, theft from the pharaoh is punishable by execution. He would not be foolish enough, he loves his wife too much to expose her to something like that," Neti remarked, they are happy and comfortable.

"And your parents?" Shabaka chanced to ask.

"Definitely not!" Neti firmly decreed, "I have helped my father process bodies, there were only natron, cloth and sawdust ever placed within them."

"I should buy you a beer, I'm actually excited by our discovery."

"So you will be following up on that instead?" Neti demurely asked.

Shabaka looked at her, halting before turning to grasp her shoulders." I made a promise to help you find your parents' killer. I am a man of my word, however I suspect their deaths may be connected to this: maybe your father discovered something and was going to report it," Shabaka reasoned, "it would be reason enough to kill him."

"We should tell the mayor," Neti grudgingly replied.

"No!" Shabaka said firmly, "This stays between us. The pharaoh was very specific in stating that I am to function independently from the mayor, and closing the gates could be obstructive for following this. But let's hope it takes a few more days before the Vizier's man returns."

Chapter 4

The half moon hung low over the plains of Thebes, its glow casting a gray glow against the city walls, with the light barely reaching the streets. The city's inhabitants had long since gone to bed, rendering the streets still in the early morning hours, allowing him to move about freely without fear of being discovered. He moved unrestricted across the rooftops as he made his way to his destination, once or twice having needed to slip the flint knife back in place under his dark robe. It was always on his side in the evenings, having become his constant companion.

He finally came to the desired rooftop kitchen, his intended destination, and made his way down the stairs and into the home. Its arrangement was familiar to him as he moved about it with ease. It was neat, as he knew it would be, and he made his way to the one small table where he knew he would find a lamp. He lit it and turned for the bedchamber, carefully moving the fabric from the doorway to allow him entry. He moved to the side of his bed, once again reaching for the knife that seemed to slip, before coming to a halt.

The pale glow from the lamp shone over the sleeping form, and he reached out towards her. It had been so long since she had last visited with him, her attentions having gone to the Nubian prefect as of late. The dark skinned man did not deserve her attentions, she was too good a person, with too an important part, to spend her time with one so low, so unimportant. But that would soon be righted, he would soon be a god: and she was going to help him with the powers in her heart ...

A rattling noise nearby caused him to suddenly withdraw his hand from her. He glanced about the room, before stepping away from the bed, moving to check the surrounding areas. He slipped through the doorway, blowing out the lamp as he went. He progressed up the stairs and towards the small altar, expecting to find someone there. He chided himself for not checking the other bedchamber: for all he knew the Nubian prefect could be there ... the dark skinned man was of a formidable size, which is why he had not bothered to do away with him yet. He knew his limitations when it came to his physical strength and agility, and the prefect was a fully trained soldier, that could easily overpower him. However, once he was a god, he would vanquish the man, do away with the threat he posed. His hands clasped at the thought of the man's familiarity with her, as he descended the stairs and returned to the main room. He placed the lamp back in its place before making for the kitchen: the eastern horizon was already lightening: there would be another time to see her.

By mid morning, the Northern Gates of Thebes were congested by merchants and travelers alike: with the steady rise in temperature doing little to appease those awaiting authorization. Both visitors and merchants took offence at the guards' sudden insistence on checking their wares and querying them as to their intended destination. Scribes noted down the larger merchants' movements and loads, as smaller merchants and arriving travelers were allowed to pass through, almost undisturbed.

A runner arrived at the gates and was halted by one of the guards, gruffly demanding, "Reason for your visit?" whilst looking over the darkly tanned runner.

"I bring scrolls from the Anum," the man quickly replied, lifting a scroll bearing the seal of Anum.

"All documents originating from the courts are to be taken to the mayor's house," the guard commanded, before indicating to one of the younger recruits to step closer. "Take this runner to the mayor," the guard instructed, and the young recruit nodded his head in acquiescence, before turning to lead the way for the runner.

Once they were a few yards from the gates, the Anum runner spoke up, "Why the need for guards at the gate?"

The young recruit slowed his pace, for a moment looking towards the visitor, before answering, "The prefect stipulated that we are regulate all activities at the gates, by checking all incoming and outgoing merchandize, as well as persons leaving the city: there is a killer on the loose, and he does not want the man to escape."

"You are not concerned for your safety?" the runner asked, as they once again picked up their pace.

"No, there is no reason to. It seems that the killer only targets persons who have had contact with the Witch of the Dead," the young guard stated, adding, "That is why everyone in town will not go anywhere near her, except the prefect; he does not seem too concerned for his safety," the young recruit apathetically added.

"I will make sure to leave at the soonest convenience," the runner replied.

"Come, the mayor's house is just along here," the young recruit said, once again picking up his pace.

They entered the mayor's home, with his footman showing them into a gathering room, where the mayor was seated with some of the town elders and merchants.

"We do not see the need for our merchandize to be checked on leaving the city," one of the merchants spoke up, glancing around the room in hope of gaining espousal from the others seated there.

"He is correct," another added, "yesterday it took my men nearly half a day to exit the city with goods bound for Karnak. The trip has never taken more than half a day in its entirety, with the donkeys back in their stalls before the midday mealtime."

"He makes a point," Ma-Nefer remarked, "Few of us can afford delays like that, especially when we transport foodstuffs to the temple that might spoil: the gods will not be exultant at receiving rotten offerings." Many of those in the room nodded their heads in agreement, murmuring amongst themselves.

"The prefect has assured me that the checks will be halted once the murderer is caught," the mayor replied lifting his hands slightly in an attempt to calm those within the room. "It is better than closing the city gates entirely, and barring all papyrus boats from mooring here," the mayor firmly added; his words had everyone in the room fall silent, glancing at one another. "This arrangement allows for you to continue your trade,' the mayor concluded, before lifting his gaze to his house servant, noticing the new arrivals and demanding, "What do you want?"

The young recruit bowed his head in greeting, before speaking, "A runner from Anum has arrived at the Northern Gates with documents: I have brought him here as instructed, Sir."

The mayor looked at the man standing next to the recruit, before brusquely demanding, "State your business. Can you not see I am busy?"

The runner shifted slightly on his feet, before hesitantly speaking up, "I bring documents from Anum."

"Well don't just stand there spreading roots like a papyrus, hand them over!" the mayor demanded, holding his hand out for the scroll.

The runner hesitated for a moment, before replying, "But these documents are not for you."

The mayor glared at the man, before indicating to the room of people, "You see these people: they are here complaining to me about the restrictions of movement imposed on this town." The mayor's words had the runner look around the room, noticing the hostile faces.

"At this moment, everything coming into and going out of Thebes is under scrutiny. So, hand those documents over," the mayor commanded.

The runner nodded his head and stepped closer, holding out the scroll towards the mayor. "Here," he said as he placed the scroll in the mayor's bulbous hand.

The mayor looked at the scroll for a moment, before breaking the seal in front of those present.

The runner made to object but was cautioned by the recruit, and instead remained silent, as the mayor opened the scroll, looking it over, before handing it to his appointed scribe to read, demanding, "Tell those in the room what it is about," whilst unswervingly looking at Ma-Nefer.

The scribe took the scroll, reading through it before speaking up. "It is an official document certifying that Neti-Kerty may practice as an embalmer," the scribe replied before once again rolling up the scroll and handing it to the mayor.

"That cannot be," one of the elders spoke up in protest. "She will forsake their souls."

The runner for a moment looked towards the young recruit, as another elder spoke up, "The witch of the dead cannot be allowed to practice."

The mayor took the scroll from his scribe, before turning towards the runner, commanding, "You are dismissed."

The young man looked about the room, before replying, uncertainly, "But I am to deliver that to the overseer directly."

"I will see that he gets it," the mayor dismissingly replied. "You can go."

The young recruit indicated to the runner that they should leave, and the runner reluctantly swayed on his feet.

"Well, what are you waiting for?" the mayor demanded, "get along with you," he commanded, before turning back to the elders with him: placing the scroll next to him on the floor.

Neti-Kerty was seated at the grinding stone, in the process of grinding wheat for her bread. She looked at her supply of wheat, judging that she would soon need to go to the market to get some more. She halted her actions for a moment: contemplating what excess vegetables she had in the garden, and which she could possibly trade for more wheat. She did not want to spend any more of her money, and bartering her access vegetables seemed the most viable option. Her mother had planted enough food to feed their family, however it was excessive now.

She took another handful of grain from the sack, casting it into the hollowed out stone, once again taking hold of the grinding stone and rolling it with practiced ease: she had to make extra bread as offering to the gods, feeling guilty for having neglected her offerings and daily prayers.

The rhythmic grinding of the grain between the stones soothed her nerves. It was an activity she has always found comforting to do: one she preferred above weaving or drawing water. Her mother had insisted upon her acquiring all these skills, however she found weaving to be the most difficult, often making mistakes and having to undo and reset everything, where the rhythmic grinding soon had her humming whilst she worked the grain into fine flour.

She was just about to add another handful of wheat to the grinding stones, when a knock sounded at the door. Neti rose from her position, dusting off her hands before making for the door as the second, and more insistent, knock sounded. Her heart skipped a beat at the thought of it being Shabaka, as it had been a few days since she had last seen him. There had been no murders since their visit to the main Per-Nefer chambers, and he had since needed to focus his attention on other matters.

She opened the door, smiling warmly until she noticed an unknown man standing there. He was dressed in pale threadbare clothing that was stained in places, suggesting him to be a slave of some sorts. He swayed from side to side, nervously looking about him whilst remaining at a distance from her.

"Can I help you?" Neti asked as she stepped fully into the doorway.

"Ugh. Yes." The man started uncertainly, once again looking about him, before continuing, "I have come to collect monies owing to Kadurt."

Neti looked at him for a moment, her gaze then dropping to the ground as she tried to recollect if there was any mention of a Kadurt in her father's will, before she shook her head and returned her stare to the man. "I'm sorry, but I do not recall owing him anything."

The slave once again glanced around, before hesitantly pulling out a scroll, replying, "According to this, Kadurt made a payment to your father for his burial. However, with your father's death, he now requests the return of his money, as he no longer has need for the services from you."

Neti looked at the man in confusion. "I know nothing of these arrangements," she stated, before glancing at the document he held, "Could I have a look at that document?"

The slave carefully handed her the scroll, maintaining some distance from her, and watched as she unrolled the scroll and read it. "I will need to speak to Suten Anu regarding this matter, he handles my father's concerns," Neti stated as she rolled up the scroll.

The slave looked at her in dismay, before bemoaning, "I am to return to Kadurt with payment, he insisted so,"

"We can go to Suten Anu's offices now," Neti offered. "I cannot make such a large payment without knowing the estate's matters." Neti's heart was pounding, knowing that she might not have sufficient funds to cover the requested amount.

The slave looked hesitantly at her, then at the scroll she held, remembering the beating his master had promised him if he did not succeed, before finally nodding in agreement."We can go."

The slave stepped back and allowed Neti to step from the house. Once she had closed the door, he gestured for her to precede him, allowing some distance between them before following her to the old scribe's offices.

Their walk to Suten Anu's offices was not long, and many of those they passed on the road gazed after them in bewilderment.

Neti entered Suten Anu's office, and the elderly scribe looked up at her, smiling warmly on recognition until he noticed the man with her, and instead of greeting her he asked, "Neti, dear child, what is this?" whilst indicating the man who came to a standstill behind her.

"Good day Suten, I apologize for intruding, however this man claims that I owe Kadurt payment," Neti stated gesturing toward the man standing behind her. "I need you to confirm if it is so," Neti concluded, holding the scroll out for the elderly man to take.

Suten Anu rose from his seat, stepping round his desk before taking the scroll from her. He opened it and read through before looking at the man, declaring, "I know nothing of these arrangements, and I deal with all the estate's matters," before once again looking over the document, and asking, "why did your owner not submit this to me the morning after the embalmer's death?"

When the slave failed to answer, Suten Anu lifted his gaze, looking pointedly at the man, who stuttered, "I do not know," in reply, adding, more firmly, "I only know that he demands payment, today."

Suten Anu again looked at the papyrus scroll, for a moment considering what in the estate would cover such an exorbitant amount.

"I do not know of any practice in which one makes payment for his burial arrangements before their death. I know that many acquire riches and possessions for their burial beforehand, but I have never heard of any paying an embalmer until his services are needed," Suten Anu started, halting for a moment as he studied some of the hieroglyphics detailing payments. "I will need to consult with the overseer regarding the legality of this matter, as a hundred-and-twenty Debben is an exorbitant amount for such services, especially since no mention is made for the provision of a sarcophagus."

"But Kadurt demands payment now," the man insisted, his distress evident in his voice, causing Suten Anu to look at him before nodding his head.

"Your owner will beat you if you return with nothing," Suten remarked, causing the man to incline his head in reply. He turned to his desk and extracted a sheet of paper, before turning to Neti. "Until such time as this matter is resolved, we will pledge the wooden door as partial payment," he stated looking at Neti, who acknowledged his reply. He turned his attention to the slave. "It is worth at least twenty-five Debben,"

"But he demands full payment now," the slave insisted as Suten Anu started scribing on a piece of paper.

"There are few who could afford such a payment outright: I dare say even the pharaoh would think twice before making such a payment." Suten Anu paused from his writings and regarded the slave, "Until the actual legality of this matter, and the payment for these services has been corresponded, there will be no further payments."

"But the money is due him," the slave complained.

"And I dare say he did not make this payment in haste, it would have to be corresponded first," Suten said, turning for the door, "I will accompany you for the collection of the door."

Neti stepped from Suten Anu's office, and fell in step with him as they returned to her home. "I apologize for this," she said as they walked along the road.

"Do not fuss dear child, it is why I am here," he replied dismissively.

"You will speak with Marlep about this?" Neti questioned, turning to look at the slave who followed at a safe distance.

"I will go see him, but you know nothing of these arrangements?"

"No, I do not. But my father has always handled our income, I do not know much about it," Neti honestly replied. "However a hundred-and-twenty Debben is a lot of money. I cannot remember any time where we had such wealth."

"That is exactly why this requires further inquiries," Suten remarked, as they approached Neti's home, then he asked whilst indicating to the door, "You have something to place in the doorway?"

Neti nodded her head in response, before adding, "I can use the reed-mat in the kitchen, until I have time to make something more suitable."

Suten Anu helped the slave to remove the door, before handing him the newly scribed scroll, bidding the man farewell, before turning to Neti and asking, "Have you heard from the Anum regarding your papers?"

"No I have not," Neti dejectedly replied. "I think he may have turned down my application, and if that is the matter, I will not be able to buy out of my marriage to Ma-Nefer even if the Kenbet rule in my favor, especially since this—" Neti said indicating the door.

"Let us first see if the documents are authentic," Suten Anu said.

"You think they may not be?" Neti asked in surprise.

" Kadurt is known for forging documents: although it has never been substantiated, or any of the matters taken to the Kenbet for assessment. He is not the first person to attempt to gain from others' misfortune. And I dare say your father was known to be highly proficient in his profession, which makes it very difficult to contest such an arrangement," Suten Anu calmly replied, before smiling warmly at Neti. "But until such time as its legitimacy is confirmed, I suggest we return to our duties: as your flour will not grind itself."

"How did you know?" Neti quickly asked, with a slight tilt of her head..

Suten Anu raised a finger towards her head, "There is some in your wig."

Neti reached up a little, brushing as she replied, "I should have cleaned up before approaching you."

"Whatever for my dear? For this old fool? I dare say I'm not your prefect friend," Suten Anu was quick to josh her.

"You are not an old fool," Neti was quick to decree in return. "You are a very wise man, and a true friend," she sincerely replied, before her voice dipped slightly, "besides Shabaka is just a person I help, I do not think he sees me in such a way."

"Sometimes my child, I think we spent too much time educating you: that we have taken from you the skills to recognize when a man is taken by you."

Neti shook her head at that. "I'm certain he already has a wife, and children. He is too good a person not to. Also, he is only here by order of the pharaoh."

Suten Anu looked at her for a moment, before reaching for her shoulder, "Have you asked him my dear, it is not unknown for Nubians to have more than one wife."

"I could not do that!" Neti quickly replied, "And I would not want to be one of many either."

Suten Anu nodded his head at that. "That I can well understand my child: but like you I need to return to my work. I will see to this and let you know in the morning." And with that, he took his leave of her.

Ma-Nefer stepped from the mayor's home, a smug grin on his face as a sense of glee filled him: thinking that it was all starting to fall in place. He swung his carrier over his shoulder, checking its contents, before moving along the street, sidestepping a woman returning from the river and her annoying children that were running about unchecked. He could not understand why some would want to burden themselves with children, they only cost more to feed and made no real contribution to the household until they were weaned and trained.

He sidestepped a young boy, knocking him to the ground in the process, and did not even bother to turn around to check when the child started crying. He finally turned onto a derelict path, and glanced about to ensure that no one had followed him, before continuing further along it.

He entered a darkened passageway and lit the lamp that was left at the entrance, before continuing onto the abandoned Per-Nefer chamber. He held up the lamp as he entered the room, casting it in a pale glow, whilst looking around: sneering when he saw the canopic jar standing on the platform. He walked over to the platform, placing the lamp on it before reaching out and stroking the engraved insignia on the jar. He lifted its lid to check on the contents, before closing the jar and placing his carry bag on the platform. Reaching into it he extracted an empty canopic jar and placed it on the platform, before placing the filled one into the bag. He then stepped from the platform and turned to check on the natron supply: knowing that it would be a whole moon cycle before the next shipment arrived. Satisfied with the supply, he returned to the platform to collect up his carrier bag, carefully situating the jar inside it, before reaching for the lamp and exiting the chamber.

He made his way back to his trading post as quickly as his feet could convey his bulk, and once there, he secluded himself in the back of one of the storage areas. He extracted the canopic jar from the bag, looking it over, smiling smugly as he placed it upon the shelf with the others.

The quarter moon was slowly sinking away as the gray-light of dawn started to creep over the horizon. In the still streets, a bulkily dressed figure moved along the path, glancing about to ensure that no one saw his progress. He came to a halt in front of a doorway, for a moment glancing confused at the reed mat covering it. However, he pushed it out of the way before stepping inside.

The rooms within were dark, with only the outlines of furniture visible. The man made his way to the small table on which the lamp stood, using the flint stones next to it to light it.

He looked about the room as the lamp cast a low glow, before making his way to her sleeping chamber. He reached toward the fabric partition, moving it out of the way, before reaching under his cloak and resetting the object hidden from view, and continuing to her bedside. He watched her sleep for a moment in the pale light, his heart feeling heavy as a weighty sigh escaped him. He placed the lamp next to the bed, before reaching out toward her, having almost reached her when her eyes shot open.

He immediately smacked his hand over her mouth to prevent her from screaming. Her hand instantly reached for his, gripping it to pull it away, as her eyes enlarged in recognition. He pushed down harder in order to keep his hand in place. His grip tightening, his fingers pushing up against her nose, making breathing almost impossible: causing her to struggle against him.

Neti shook her head in an attempt to dislodge his hand, her heart pounding faster as her body's demand for oxygen increased. Little dots started blurring her vision as her lungs burnt in need of air. She opened her jaw as far as she could, once again shaking her head before clamping down hard on whatever part of his hand she could. He screamed in objection and jerked his hand away, knocking over the lamp and dropping the bulky object from beneath his cloak as he stumbled away from the bed, clasping his one hand in the other, hissing in pain.

Neti immediately moved, reaching for the earthenware pot that stood next to her bed, lifting it, before flinging it at him, shouting, "Asim, Get out!"

Asim ducked, and the pot shattered against the wall behind him. The same moment the spilled oil from the lamp caught fire. He regained his feet: stepping on the shards of pottery that sheared through the skin of his soles, as he turned to limp as speedily as possible from the room, leaving a trail of bloody footprints in his wake.

Neti rose from the bed moving as swiftly as she could, and started to put out the fire as the oil continued to spread over the floor. Some commotion from her doorway caused her to look up, recognizing her one neighbor, who appeared stunned by the sight, then turned from the room.

Shabaka rushed toward Neti's home, his heart racing as he hurried through the slowly awakening streets: The young boy having summonsed him having only mentioned a disturbance at her home. However, his stomach churned when he turned into the street leading up to her house and saw the people gathered outside, his steps for a moment faltering.

He halted for a moment outside her door, confused, as he looked at her doorway, glancing around to ensure that he was indeed at the correct house, before pushing aside the mat to enter. He glanced about the room, his heart dropping to his feet, swallowing against the bile that rose in his throat at the sight of the bloody prints leading from her room. A numb sensation took hold of him as he reluctantly made his way toward the doorway. He knew what to expect, but was uncertain if he could face what lay behind the fabric partition. The smell of burnt oil and reeds filled his nostrils as he took a deep breath to steady his nerves, before moving the fabric out of his way, already chiding himself for not having checked up on her recently.

The room was empty: the broken shards of the pot lay next to the wall, with a black charred patch on the floor next to the bed. A bolt of relief flushed through him on sight of the room's disarray, thankful that he was not greeted with a bloody sight and her mutilated body. He froze an instant later, registering her absence from the room and seemingly the house: instantly resisting the thought that the killer could have taken her. His stomach turned at that thought, for he had no idea as to where to look for her, or the killer.

A noise from the other room drew his attention, and caused him to exit it, halting dead in his tracks at the sight of her. "Neti," he hoarsely gasped, causing her to look at him, moments before closing the distance between them and drawing her into an embrace. He finally found his voice and hoarsely exclaimed, "By Ra! I thought he had gotten you."

He held her for several moments before drawing back slightly to look at her, asking, "Are you okay? He did not hurt you?"

Neti shook her head at that, her gaze remaining lowered. Shabaka looked her over, noting the strip of bandage around her one wrist, and took hold of her arm, demanding, "What happened?"

"I hurt it while putting out the fire," Neti reluctantly replied, pulling her arm from his grasp and stepping from him.

"Did you see who it was?" Shabaka questioned, stepping closer to her, not wanting too great a distance separating them.

Neti nodded her head in response, pursing her lips as her gaze remained fixed to the floor.

"Did you recognize him?" Shabaka hurriedly demanded.

Neti again gave a nod of her head.

"Who was it?" Shabaka quickly demanded, watching as she swallowed.

"Asim," Neti weakly replied.

"Asim!" Shabaka exclaimed, shocked.

Neti simply confirmed.

"That's it," Shabaka heatedly started, "From now on every guard will search for him until he is found!" He moved towards the door, halting dead in his tracks when Suten Anu entered the room.

"Neti," the elderly scribe called to her, "I just heard."

Neti instinctively moved into the older man's arms, and Shabaka felt himself envying the instinctive reaction: clenching his fists and clamping his jaw as the elderly man held her close.

Neti stepped back a few moments later, and looked at the scribe, who glanced around the room.

"I dare say he had easy access, it is just strange for it to occur now," Suten Anu started before looking at Neti.

"Why do you say that?" Neti hesitantly asked.

"Ah, it is just me, being an old man," Suten dismissed it, "but I cannot understand why he would come back for you now."

"Possibly because he needed the business that her father provided with his death," Shabaka spoke up, his voice gruff, failing to hide his discontent.

"I do not follow," Suten said turning his attention towards the Nubian.

"Asim was here this morning," Shabaka stated flatly.

"Asim?" Suten Anu returned in disbelief. "But he would never harm Neti. He has watched her grow up." Suten turned to look at Neti for conformation, and Neti just nodded her head in response. "I find that hard to believe."

"Well believe it or not, we have to find the man," Shabaka firmly decreed, "before he hurts anyone else."

"Yes that is understandable," Suten replied nodding, before turning to Neti and gripping her shoulders, "And here I was hoping that this would be a day for celebration."

"Celebration?" Neti asked, confused.

"I received word from the Kenbet late yesterday," he started, noticing how both Neti and Shabaka listened with renewed interest. "They have ruled that if you are capable of settling the outstanding amount to Ma-Nefer, that the stipulation in the will can be negated."

"You mean I no longer have to marry him?" Neti enthused.

"I have sent a footman to him to collect the records of what your father owed him, also to inform him of the Kenbet's ruling: he should arrive there shortly.

"I do not think he will be pleased with that," Neti replied.

Ma-Nefer was just sitting down to his breakfast when the old scribe's footman arrived, demanding to see him. The man entered the room and nodded his head in greeting before holding out a scroll for the portly man to take. Ma-Nefer took the scroll and opened it, before turning to one of the female attendants, instructing, "You, go call Zahar for me," then scrunched the scroll together, before placing it to the side.

The woman nodded her head in response and set off to call the old Nubian slave, whilst Ma-Nefer went about his breakfast.

Zahar entered the room with his head lowered, greeting, "You called, Master."

"Read that," Ma-Nefer commanded, pointing toward the scroll, then continuing with his meal.

The Nubian picked up the scroll and opened it, his eyes moving over the hieroglyphics, before starting, "In accordance with the Kenbet ruling, all records of outstanding debt, and monies owed by the Neith estate, are to be forwarded to the estate overseer, Suten Anu, for payment. The courts have ruled that if the estate is capable of settling all debts, that the heir will no longer be required to fulfill the obligations set in the final section of the testament."

"What!" Ma-Nefer exclaimed rising from his seat. "That cannot be!" His exclamation sent all the slaves present scurrying in various directions.

Ma-Nefer turned to face the old Nubian slave: who had also moved from his side, having dropped the scroll in his haste. He glanced past him at Thoth, before angrily demanding, "What are you laughing at you useless piece of flesh!" and reaching for his whip. The slaves all scattered in various directions, as he swung it, aiming it at Thoth, exclaiming, "You who is the sickest bastard of them all," as the whip connected with Thoth's back. Thoth screamed in pain as the whip tore through his flesh. Ma-Nefer drew back the whip, before swinging it again, "You, stupid idiot, that covets his own sister!" the man continued as the whip once again came down on Thoth's back, drawing more blood. "You are not man enough for any woman, you have nothing to offer them, you are nothing but a useless slave," he continued as another strike stuck home.

129

Thoth fell to the ground in pain long before Ma-Nefer lowered the whip, "That will teach you not to laugh at your Master," Ma-Nefer wheezed before looking about the room, then at the Nubian slave who had remained at the doorway. "Well get him out of here!" he commanded, huffing slightly, before turning back to the footman, "I'll send the information to your master, at my convenience."

The footman bowed his head in acknowledgement before turning from the room.

Zahar and one of the other slaves carried Thoth's battered body to the sleeping barracks, and one of the female slaves followed: bearing a bowl of water and cloths.

They placed him on his sleeping mat and the woman kneeled next to him, and carefully started tending to his wounds.

"Neti?" Thoth whimpered, at the woman's touch.

"No Thoth it is I, Yani. Rest now, and let me see to your wounds," the woman said as she set to clearing the blood, wincing slightly as Thoth jerked beneath her touch.

"It is not true," Thoth muttered.

"What?" Yani gently asked.

"Neti is not my sister, she loves me," he murmured.

"Shh now Thoth, do not upset yourself," Yani replied as she reached for the salve Neti had made for Thoth: they all used it on their welts. She nodded her head at the thought of the young woman escaping their condemnation. "She is lucky to escape this," the woman softly said, her voice portraying her longing for freedom as she started smoothing the salve over Thoth's wounds, wondering if there would be enough to tend to all of them. Yani stopped for a moment and looked at the young man before her, her heart feeling heavy as he started humming quietly: a tune she had been told he had hummed since a child. She would go see Neti later, and ask her for more of the salve: the young woman had never complained when they requested more, and was always willing to help them, especially Thoth.

Chapter 5

The steadily rising sun's reflection played on the waters of the Nile as a fish eagle motionlessly hung in mid-air, its wingtips playing in the breeze as it floated over the river's surface, before suddenly swooping down, its claws clasping at the surface as it lifted a fish from the water. Its powerful wings beat upwards to lift it from the water's surface before it flew into the distance.

Crocodiles lay sunning themselves on the riverbank, lazily gazing out over the water, whilst wild Egyptian geese and ducks moved along the reeds foraging for insects and food.

Further upstream, a ferry was moored. Guards looked on as bearers loaded and secured the crates containing the pharaoh's gems, along with other goods and taxes bound for his palace in Pi-Ramesses. Scribes commissioned by Ramesses II, for the inscription of the Ramesseum walls and chambers, also made their way to the ferry, in order to return to their work on the western bank after their day of rest.

Not far from there, women were doing their washing, many of them chanting and singing familiar songs, whilst others drew water for their homes, caught up with the latest gossip or bartered goods and services. Children cheerfully ran amok, playing and chasing one another along the lower grasses, whilst their older siblings searched the reeds and long grasses for duck and wild geese eggs.

A high pitched, blood curling scream sounded from the nearby reeds, causing everyone in the immediate area to halt their activities, mid action and look in its direction. A mother, having recognized her daughters squeal, bustled toward the sound. She pushed through the reeds until she reached her child, gasping at the sight before her: flies buzzed about the half eaten body of a man, his flesh already starting to rot, with the stench steadily increasing.

Others also pushed through the reeds and came to a halt, slightly behind the woman, many visibly gagging as they saw the body. One of the mothers turned to her son and told him to call the guard, and the young boy turned and ran for the gates.

Some time later, the guard situated at the gate, along with his recruit, pushed through the gathered group and came to a sudden halt. He took one look at the body and signalled for his recruit to summons Shabaka to the scene.

As the young recruit left, he started ushering people away from the body, telling them to keep well clear of the area.

Shabaka made his way to the river, already disgruntled by the morning's earlier events. He did not feel up to dealing with the half-eaten body of a man, who had carelessly gone into the river whilst crocodiles were about. There were certain areas of the river that were considered out of bounds, dangerous, and most citizens avoided them. However there were always those who tempted fate.

He stepped past the gathering crowd and came to a standstill next to the guard, looking down at the body. Both arms and most of the man's lower body had been consumed, with only his upper chest and head remaining. Shabaka gawped at the body for a moment, noting the marking on the side of his head, before speaking, "Is he not one of the guards assigned to the North Gate?"

The guard looked at the man, before nodding his head, "Yes, his name is Apopois ... but he had been sent to Abydos on an errand for the mayor," the man concluded.

"It looks like he has then met a very untimely death," Shabaka replied looking around the area, before continuing, "he possibly came to bathe after his trip, and got dragged into the river by a crocodile." Shabaka moved slightly to the side, checking between the reeds, before adding, "There is no way we can tell how long he has been here, only that it has been some time, due to the stench."

Shabaka stood looking at the body for a while, something about the situation troubled him. Although he had at first thought it was someone who had carelessly wandered into the river, he knew that no guard, even in the dead of night, would enter an area considered to be unsafe. Also, the body was not far from where the citizens daily moved. Also if he had been attacked by a crocodile, it would be unlikely for them to even find a body.

He also knew that after the morning's events, it would be unlikely that Neti would to be willing to have a look at another body. However, he would have liked her thoughts on it.

Just then, a low humming started amongst some of the women gathered not far from there, some escalating into heated discussions causing him to turn in their direction, his gaze following the direction of their stares.

Neti was on her way down to the river, carrying a pile of laundry as she stepped along the well-trodden path. He knew she would once again be rearranging her home, after the morning's invasion, however he could not pass up on the opportunity.

He summonsed one of the recruits and instructed him to summons Neti, and then became utterly frustrated when the man looked at him in question, obviously unwilling to approach the woman. Shabaka then turned to one of the nearby children, whose mother was about to object when Shabaka glared at her, and requested of the boy to beckon Neti for him. The young boy quickly ran toward Neti and delivered the message, and Shabaka watched as she turned to look in their direction, waving her hand in greeting before following the boy.

"We meet again," Neti said as she approached. The group of onlookers parted as she moved toward him.

"I need you to have a look at a body for me," Shabaka said indicating over his shoulder.

"I can smell it," Neti replied, wrinkling her nose slightly, "where is it?"

"In between the reeds," Shabaka returned, turning around to point her in the right direction.

Neti placed her woven reed basket of washing on the ground, before replying, "Okay, let's have a look," and followed Shabaka to the body.

On nearing it, she tilted her head before bending down and eventually dropping onto her haunches. She placed her hand on what remained of the man's shoulder and shifted the body slightly onto its side, looking at the patterns there, before saying, "He wasn't killed by a crocodile."

"But he's half eaten,' the one guard spoke up.

Neti continued to look at the body, before explaining. "Crocodiles will eat almost anything that floats on the river, even rotting meat.' She looked up at the guard, "His arms and legs would have been torn off first as they are the easiest to dismember. The lower half of the body was consumed because it holds the most meat, also because it is easy to rip off."

The young Guard looked at her in shock, for a moment appearing about to be ill.

"These marks here," Neti said pointing to pattering on the body's back, "are inconsistent with the death."

Neti turned her attention towards Shabaka, before stating, "He was dead before ending up in the river."

"How can you be so sure?" the guard asked in disbelief.

Neti turned to look at the man, before answering, "If he was killed by a crocodile, the blood would not have gathered on this side of the body." She then lifted the body slightly and indicated to the marks on the back, before continuing, "You see these dark marks, they mean that his heart stopped and the blood sank to that side, because he was lying on it."

"So his body was thrown into the river as a means of disposing of it," Shabaka added, "being that they would eat it, but how did it end up here."

Neti looked around her, before speaking up, "He could have been dragged up here by a younger crocodile, one who cannot yet hold its ground with the larger ones downstream. Most of the desirable meat has been picked off it, but it will be enough for a youngster and a few buzzards to pick at," Neti concluded, then ran her fingers along the spine and neck, before feeling over the skull. "His neck was not broken, but he has been struck on the head with something," she declared.

"So he was definitely murdered?"

"Yes, had he been killed by a crocodile his body would not look like this."

"So I have another murder on my hands," Shabaka sighed dejectedly, adding, "Like we do not have enough of those already."

"But why would anyone want to kill a guard?" Neti asked as she rose from her haunches, adding, "He protects the city and its people, there should be no reason to just kill him."

Shabaka turned toward her, asking outright, "Do you not know him?"

"No, not really," Neti replied, and continued once she saw Kemba's confusion, "I have seen him when I pass through the Northern Gate on my way to Karnak, but I don't know him."

"Is his heart still there?" Shabaka asked looking at the body.

"Yes, his lungs are flat, and most of his heart is still there."

"Most of his heart?"

"I think the fish and crocodiles may have eaten part of it," Neti wearily answered.

"So we can rule out the heart killer," Shabaka started in frustration, adding, "and I have no idea how to start looking for this one either."

"I would look along the river bank, see if there's any other pieces lying about," Neti shrugged, adding, "maybe you could find where he was thrown into the river."

Shabaka looked at her, tilting his head slightly before replying, "I'll get some of the guards to do it, and to collect anything suspicious they find." Then he indicated for her to precede him from the body, asking, "Would you be able to come by the Guard House tomorrow and have a look at whatever we find?"

"Certainly," Neti replied as she reached for her basket of washing, lifting it and resting it against her hip, before adding, "but I will have to go to the market first."

Shabaka simply nodded, before replying, "I will not detain you any longer, for I am certain you desire to finish your chores."

He watched her move from him, his attention drawn to the men coming in his direction. Once they were all there, he turned to them, commanding, "I want you to divide into two groups. The first is to search between here and Karnak. The second is to search between here and the ferry docks. I want you to pick up anything that does not belong to the river and return it to the guard house."

The guards nodded in agreement, then set off in opposing directions whilst Shabaka and two others remained there, checking between the reeds.

In the darkened corner of a beer house, Ma-Nefer sat waiting for Kadurt and his men to arrive. He glared at the servant girl who brought him some beer, when she asked him if he would need anything else, and returned his gaze to the doorway as she took her leave of him.

A short while later Kadurt and two of his men stepped into the beer house, looking about for a moment before spotting Ma-Nefer and making his way towards the man.

"You're late!" Ma-Nefer grumpily stated.

"Oh, and what has you so grumpy so early in the morning?" Kadurt ribbed the portly man, "Not enough meat with your breakfast this morning?"

Ma-Nefer just glared at the Kadurt in response, and the man quickly became serious.

"I just received news that Neti-Kerty is allowed by the Kenbet to buy herself out of her betrothal," Ma-Nefer bitterly replied, looking pointedly at the man.

"That was not unexpected," Kadurt relied, shrugging his shoulders.

"No," Ma-Nefer said dangerously low, placing his beer on the floor next to his seat, adding "it was not." He then moved swiftly, grabbing the man by the neck, his grip unrelenting as he shouted in the man's face, "What was to be expected, was that you would deplete her assets so that she had no means of purchasing herself out of the agreement!"

Kadurt's men made a move to help him, but halted when Ma-Nefer tightened his grip on Kadurt's neck, stepping back slightly, when Ma-Nefer continued, "It was a very simple task, need I not remind you—lucrative for you as well."

"Only because you did not want any of the furnishings," Kadurt managed to choke out, before Ma-Nefer thrust him back, letting go of his neck; Kadurt took a few deep breaths before gaining his feet.

"You had better make sure she cannot buy out of her betrothal, or you may find it difficult doing business in this town," Ma-Nefer threatened in a low voice before reaching for his beer.

"She has already made a sizable payment towards the claimed debt," Kadurt replied, still rubbing his neck.

"Yes the door, I heard." Ma-Nefer deadpanned.

"It's worth at least twenty Debben, I cannot demand the rest so soon. The old scribe will once again interfere," Kadurt explained.

Ma-Nefer took a sip of his beer, looking the man over, before firmly stating, "I don't care what you need to do, just make certain that she cannot buy her way out of marrying me."

"Why do you want her so much?" Kadurt asked in confusion, adding, "It's not like she is much of a woman." Kadurtes men jostled each other at that.

"She has skills, you idiot! Skills I have a good use for," Ma-Nefer barked, causing them all to cease their actions.

"Ah yes, that assurance of one's afterlife," Kadurt replied, adding, "it would take a witch to do that."

"Amongst other things," Ma-Nefer flatly replied, before barking, "Now go do the job I commissioned you for!"

"We still get to keep anything we take?" Kadurt asked.

"Yes, I have no need for it," Ma-Neffer angrily declared.

Shabaka stood looking toward the area of the river where he knew Neti would be, he found it difficult to be as close to her and yet not right there with her. His mind kept on drifting to her, and his gaze moved to the well-travelled path, knowing she would take it on her return to the city, and he had every intention of walking her home.

His heart started racing, when some time later she started on her way back. He started to make his way over to her, when he noticed a female slave approach her. He had become so use to people being disrespectful toward her that he was almost shocked when the woman addressed her with respect. It was the sudden stiffening of her body as she nodded her head that suddenly concerned him.

"Neti!" he called, and watched her turn to look in his direction, for a moment seeming torn in her decision. "Wait for me, I'll walk you home," he called, and was relieved when she nodded her head and waited for him with the woman slave. He glanced over the girl, frowning for a moment when she lowered her gaze

"This is Yani," Neti started, indicating with her free hand towards the woman, "she is one of Ma-Nefer's slaves." Neti hiked her washing basket up, before turning back onto the path.

"What does he want now?" Shabaka gruffly demanded, his hands already clenching into fists at the mention of the man's name.

"It is not he that needs something," Neti calmly replied as they started walking back up the path, "Yani has come to ask me for more salve. It seems Ma-Nefer was not too pleased at the news this morning, and has once again beaten Thoth."

"But that is not your concern," Shabaka firmly replied,

Neti suddenly stopped, before turning to him and stating emphatically, "Yes it is!" Her actions caused Shabaka to halt in mid stride, then turn to look at her.

"But he's nothing of you," Shabaka reasoned, before reaching out to take the basket from her, "let me."

Neti took a deep breath, and allowed him to take the basket, before speaking, "Thoth has been my friend since we were children, and I recently discovered that he is also my brother."

Shabaka looked at her in shock, shaking his head in disbelief, before replying, "That cannot be."

"It is a long and complex story, that I will explain to you some other time," Neti replied once again starting along the path, adding. "For now, Yani needs some of the salve I make."

As they neared Neti's home, Shabaka noticed a group of men waiting there, his step faltered slightly as he turned to look at her.

"Oh, no!" Neti softly spoke up, as she also noticed them.

"You know these men?" Kemas asked, concerned.

"It's Kadurt and his men. He claims that I owe him money and has probably come to collect payment," Neti replied turning her attention to the slave woman next to her, "Yani, could you summons Suten Anu for me. Tell him Kadurt is here."

The slave looked at her in fear, "You know that Ma-Nefer will beat me if he finds out I ran errands for someone, and he always finds out."

Neti looked at her for a moment, before nodding her head, replying, "I understand, I'll send Tarik. His father will not mind," She moved from the road towards a doorway.

A boy appeared in the doorway a few moments later, nodding his head before setting off down the road.

Neti returned to where Shabaka and Yani were waiting for her, then continued along the road until they reached Neti's home.

"Can I help you Kadurt?" Neti firmly asked.

"I've come for my money," the brawny man stated, adding, "you owe me a considerable amount, and I demand payment now!"

"Your claim has not been cleared with Suten Anu, therefore you must wait," Neti calmly replied.

"I have produced the scroll, containing my agreement with your father, I expect the return of my money because he is no longer capable of fulfilling his side of the agreement," Kadurt remarked, before turning and indicating to his men, adding, "my men will start to collect goods," and instructing his men to enter her home.

"You will not do that," Shabaka firmly decreed, placing Neti's basket on the ground.

"Will not do what, Nubian? She owes me money, a significant amount of money I may add, I have just come to collect it," Kadurt replied, challengingly.

It is unlawful to collect fees without a scribe present to document it," Shabaka firmly decreed, adding, "it is the most fundamental requirement set by the pharaoh."

"Well he is not here, now is he?" Kadurt challenged, snidely adding, "And I don't have time to wait for an old scribe to arrive."

"I bid you to cease your actions, or I shall have you arrested for unlawful behaviour," Shabaka warned the man.

"Taking what is rightfully mine is not unlawful," Kadurt baited him as his men started packing some of the wooden furniture outside.

"You cannot take that," Neti professed, rushing over to where the men were packing the furniture, "they were my mother's!"

One of Kadurt's men shoved her our of the way when she tried to lay claim to her mother's set of weaning frames, firmly stating, "They are Kadurt's now."

"You cannot take them," Neti pleaded, making to reach for them again.

"I can take anything of worth," Kadurt professed, "until your debt is settled."

Kadurt's men continued to remove furniture from her home, unheeding of Shabaka's command to stop.

A short while later, Suten Anu arrived, with the young boy in tow, firmly demanding, "What's going on here Kadurt?"

"I have come to claim my goods," Kadurt challenged, adding, "you, old scribe, should understand that."

"You received payment yesterday, with the rest to be paid once your claim's authenticity has been established," Suten Anu firmly stated.

"You question my claim?" Kadurt challenged, stepping toward the scribe.

"No person would make a payment of a hundred-and-twenty Debben at once," Suten Anu counter-challenged, adding, "it is too great an amount for anyone to come up with on such a short notice. You would have made payments; therefore it is only fair to allow her the same courteousy."

"And wait until all the other people she owes money to come to lay claim on the goods," Kadurt fiercely replied, adding, "then I will never see my money. I demand payment now."

"Stop your men, or you will not receive any payment," Suten decreed.

Oh, and what are you going to do to stop us?"

"I am here to make the payment," Suten Anu calmly replied, before casually adding, "unless you do not want it." His words caused Neti to turn toward him in surprise.

"And you are going to give me a hundred-and-twenty Debben?" The man asked in disbelief.

"A hundred Debben," Suten corrected, "the door your man took yesterday is worth at least twenty Debben, if not more."

"It is old, and used," Kadurt dismissed, signalling for his men to cease their actions.

"It is wood, and that alone makes it valuable," Suten decreed.

"And how do you expect to make his payment?" Kandurt once again challenged.

"Have your men return everything, and we will discuss business. I have the documents here, and it's fitting that we have the prefect here to witness this transaction."

Kadurt indicated to his men to return the furniture to the house, and Suten Anu indicated to Neti to oversee their correct placement, before drawing Shabaka and Kadurt to the side. He revealed a scroll and started to unroll it, before asking, "You can read Kadurt?" and handed the man the scroll.

Kadurt gave a nod and took it, reading rough its contents, smiling when he got to the figures.

When Neti once again stepped from the house, Suten Anu requested a quail and ink, which she turned to collect.

Suten handed the document to Shabaka to read, explaining, "Just so you understand the complexities of the agreement."

Shabaka read through the contract, slower than the other two men and had just finished when Neti arrived with the ink and quail. Sutten-Anu took the quail from her and signed his name, handing it to Kadurt and then to Shabaka, each respectively signing their names.

Kadurt called his men closer, before turning toward Suten Anu, demanding, "When will I receive my payment, old man?"

"Right now," Suten replied, producing a pouch of coins from beneath his tunic.

Neti's eyes bugged in disbelief, whilst Kadurt smiled in glee, professing, "This has been a good day for me." He took the money from Suten, and signalled for his men to follow, leaving a stunned Neti behind.

"But how?" Neti questioned in disbelief.

"Do not worry about it, my child," Suten-Anu soothingly replied.

"But my father would have told me if there was so much money," Neti remarked, a bemused look on her face..

"The money is not your father's, it is mine," Suten Anu clarified.

His words caused Neti to turn to him is shock, "But I cannot let you, that is your money that you have worked for."

"My dear child, you will be able to pay me back when you start practicing as an embalmer," Suten Anu calmly replied, "that is if his documents are not found to be illegal, or forgeries of some sort. In which case he has just made a foolish mistake in signing for payment. For not only will I be able to claim back the money, but he will be sent to the pharaoh for judgement as a forgerer and thief, and we all know that theft is punishable by death. Also I know of others who have suffered by his hand."

A slight movement off to the side drew their attention, and on seeing Yani still standing there, Neti's eyes bugged, "Yani, I am so sorry, come I will give you some of the salve," she quickly enthused, making for the house and disappearing through the doorway.

"What is she doing here?" Suten Anu asked Shabaka, indicating to the slave woman.

"Ma-Nefer has believably whipped Thoth this morning," Shabaka explained.

Suten shook his head in response, before replying, "That man has a cruel heart, Neti is best off far away from him.'

"You think she will get out of this marriage to him?" Shabaka asked as Neti and Yani exited the house.

"I will do everything in my power to prevent that marriage" Suten decreed, adding, "Neti has too many good qualities for Ma-Nefer's hand. He will turn her into a broken slave at the first opportune moment… I have seen what he is capable of, it is not a life for anyone."

Suten-Anu and Yani took their respective leave of Neti, and she then turned towards Shabaka as he asked, "You will still come by the Guard's house tomorrow to see what the men have found?"

"Yes, after I have been to the market."

Neti then gathered up her basket, and returned to her home, where she hung up the sheets she had washed earlier. The stench of bunt oil still permeated the air of her room when she entered it. She looked at the bloody prints left on the floor, her forehead furrowing as she placed her own foot next to one. Her brows shot up when she realized that they were not the same as the killer's – the killer's feet were bigger, where Asim's footprints were the same size as hers.

Neti again looked around the room, knowing that if he was not the killer there had been a definite reason for his visit. She finally noticed a scroll that had somehow managed to roll under her bed, and had luckily not caught fire.

She unrolled the scroll, placing it flat on the floor as she started to read it. Some of the hieroglyphs on it were unknown to her; however she was able to deduce that it was a list of quantities, and shipment details for various gemstones into the city.

Neti looked up from the scroll, frowning, wondering how Asim had managed to get hold of such an important document. She re-rolled the scroll and placed it in her clothing box. She would show it to Shabaka when she went to the guardhouse.

The sun was just breaching the horizon as Neti-Kerty stepped from her home. The streets were still silent as she made her way to her mother's vegetable garden just outside the town's Eastern Gate. She nodded her head in greeting to the guard on duty, and continued along the path until she came to the small portion of land her mother had worked.

A piercing whistle sounded, causing her to look in its direction, noticing a young herder gathering his goats. The animals gathered together and followed the boy as he led them away from the gardens and onto the uncultivated parts of land. A gazelle leapt up from its cover below a shrub, not far from the boy, and scurried away into the distance, the boy looking on as the animal gracefully leapt.

Neti smiled as she turned her attention back to the garden, selecting some of the melons and carobs, placing them in the hessian bag she had brought with her. Once done, she walked over to the irrigation stream, collecting one of the old water pitchers and drawing water for the garden. She carefully watered all the plants and had just returned the pitcher to its place, when some of the other gardeners appeared. Mostly they ignored her presence, and simply stepped past her and onto their own gardens, allowing her to finish up her work, unhindered.

Neti gathered up the hessian bag and made her way back into town, hoping that she would be able to exchange some of the harvest for some cloth, weaving reeds, and oil with the local shuty. Carobs were well sought after and were likely to trade easily, she was uncertain about the melons, as they were abundant and no one needed to trade for them.

Foreign shuties, and the pharaoh's grain shuty only accepted coins, and she needed to hold onto those she had until she could practice her trade; therefore she limited her trips to the market to only gather essentials.

Neti returned home to collect up her satchel and two Debben, hurriedly tidying herself before setting out to the market.

The market was as usual bustling with activity, with people moving in all directions almost simultaneously. Children ran about between fellow market goers and the various drays, displaying a variety of produce and goods, chanting and singing as they went along.

Snake charmers and acrobats entertained onlookers with their skills, as others briskly stepped past them and onto the main market place.

Most market goers were too caught up in their own activities to notice Neti, therefore she moved about with relative ease, with those who recognized her maintaining a steady distance from her, glaring to ensure she maintained her distance.

She gazed about the main market place, the variety of colors and produce almost overwhelming. The strong scent of exotic spices filled the air. Their rich yellow, ochre and red coloring drew the attention of many market goers, with various shuties boasting special breads and foods. Henna artists painted intricate designs on their patrons' hands or feet, with other various salves and cosmetics drawing attention from the younger women.

Neti moved between the drays and carts, glancing at the goods, at times halting for closer inspection. She was drawn to a dray, displaying some of the finest fabrics she had ever seen, causing her to reach out and stroke the fine fabric. The shuty smiled warmly at her, his unshaven appearance gave credence to his Byblos origin. Neti nodded her head in greeting and returned her attention toward the fabric. It was not the flax or cotton she was accustomed to, its sheer texture was soft to touch.

Neti turned her attention to the man, asking, "What fabric is this?"

"That is the finest silk in all of the East. So sheer you will not even know you are wearing anything."

"It is really beautiful," Neti replied smiling, adding, "but it is not what I require."

"You are needing cloth, yes?" the man questioned, eager to assist her.

"I need linen," Neti replied, looking at some of the other fabrics.

The man moved some of the bolts of fabric, picking up a strong and supple white fabric, before replying, "I have some right here, made from the finest cotton in all of Byblos."

Neti reached to stroke the fabric, smiling at its texture.

"Only two Debben a length," the man enthused.

Neti shook her head in regret, "It is a fine fabric, but I fear it is above my means."

The man inclined his head in understanding, and Neti moved on to the next dray.

The scent of several specialty breads wafted through the air, reminding her that she had still not eaten breakfast. She found it exceedingly difficult to attend to all the various things that required her attention, and still cook meals, and as a result limited her diet to flatbread, beer and fruit, which were easily obtainable. However, she missed her mother's cooking.

Her thoughts had her halt at a farmer's dray. There were geese, eggs and beeswax on offer, and Neti looked at the geese, but then shook her head, thinking she should rather set the dove trap if she wanted meat. Then she moved on to the cart where the pharaoh's grain shuty could be found.

The shuty looked her over for a moment, before stating, "I only accept coinage as payment."

Neti nodded her head, before requesting, "I need a hekat's worth of wheat and two hinws' worth of barely."

"That will be two kite," the shuty gruffly replied.

Neti reached into her satchel and extracted the copper debben coin, handing it to the man. At the appearance of the coin, his whole demeanor changed as he bustled to gather the requested grains. He handed her two flax bags, and eight smaller silver kite pieces.

She pocketed the small coins then placed the grain in her hessian bag and continued along the path. She met up with a local weaver a few drays further, and bartered the exchange of the carobs, melons and a kite for two lengths of fabric.

It was as she moved from the dray that a bearded man bumped into her. His hands gripped her shoulders in an attempt to steady her, profusely apologizing for the incident before moving on.

She continued along the market drays, finally halting at one bearing fresh fruits, where she bought some figs and grapes. It was when she placed the fruit in her satchel that her hand came into contact with a small scroll. She grasped it and pulled it from her satchel, looking at it in confusion, before looking about the market, seeking the bearded man that had bumped into her, thinking it his and wanting to return it. However, he was nowhere in sight.

She looked at the scroll, turning it to read the name of the recipient, and was shocked to see her own, then returned it to her satchel and turned for home.

She arrived back home and quickly placed away her purchases, then took hold of the small scroll and returned to the main living area. She unrolled it feeling an increase in her heartbeat, fearing that it could possibly be more bad news, or business requiring Suten Anu's input.

She breathed a sigh of relief when the scroll did not bear any official regalia, and started to read its contents. Her brow furrowed as she progressed through the contents. The scroll came from a party of elders claiming that the mayor and Ma-Nefer were in partnership, conspiring to keep the gates open when a killer ran loose. Also, that the mayor had not made any efforts to inform the Vizier of the murders. That in the reports to the Vizier, Pa-Nasi only included details of business agreements, harvests and taxes, and that none of the concerns voiced by the elders had been addressed. The elders were also concerned that with the discovery of a guard's body on the river bank, the city was no longer safe, especially since the mayor did not seem too alarmed by the escalating number of murders.

Neti could not understand why they would address her as there was little she could do, however she continued reading, and soon enough understood when they explained how they could not approach Shabaka, as all official documentation moving into, within and from the city was being screened by the mayor, and their notification would be seen as treason. They ended the note by requesting that she notify Shabaka and that the correct procedures could be undertaken to protect the people of Thebes.

Neti rolled up the scroll, before moving to her room to collect up the other and placing them together on her bed. She would take them with her and discuss them with Shabaka when she went to the guard house. However, first she had to set the dove traps, and have some breakfast.

The sun was already well at its zenith when Neti-Kerty stepped from her home. It had taken her longer than anticipated to prepare the barley for brewing, and she tried not to think of the list of chores that were still awaiting her attention as she walked along the hot streets, the sun-beetles were screaming and everyone moved around listlessly. Most had just consumed their main meal and were waiting for the heat of the day to dissipate before returning to their chores.

She entered the Guard House: the overwhelming smell of sweaty bodies was the first thing to register. The humming within the room suddenly halted, with most of the guards turning to look at her. Their actions caused Shabaka to turn his attention toward her, indicating for her to come approach him, adding, "I'll only be a moment, these guards are on their way to their postings," then he turned his attention back to the room and addressing them, said, "I want guards stationed at all the gates of Karnak, day and night. Everybody going into it is to be checked, and listed with a scribe." One of the guards made to object, but Shabaka added, "You do not need to physically check the bodies, only note down and regulate their movements." At his words the guards again settled. "Should anyone ask, you are to tell them that due to the desecrated bodies we have discovered, we are now regulating the movements of all bodies through Karnak, as a precaution." Shabaka looked about the room before firmly stating, "You are not to interfere with processions and services." All the guards nodded their heads in agreement.

"Those stationed at Karnak can leave, the Northern Gate guards are to remain, I wish to address them separately."

Most of the men rose from their seats and moved toward the door, with only a handful remaining. "I would like you to be more cautious until we have determined the exact reason why Apopois was murdered," Shabaka said once the others had left, adding, "You will at all times maintain a presence of two persons on duty, each change of guard will see two of the new recruits assigned to the northern and southern gates, respectively. Under no circumstances may only one guard or one recruit remain at the gate. The recruits will do your running and messaging, so there is no valid reason for you to leave your post unmanned. You will from now on also carry your weapons with you. If at any stage you are threatened, you may strike in response. They have attacked one of you, and I'm not willing to lose another guard." The men nodded their heads in agreement.

"You are dismissed," Shabaka concluded, allowing the men to leave before turning his attention towards Neti, sincerely stating, "It is good to see you."

Neti smiled in response, before replying, "I said I would come."

"Yes you did," Shabaka replied, indicating toward a draped doorway, "Everything the guards found yesterday has been placed in there. I warn you it does not smell pleasant," he added before moving the drapery out of the way.

Neti's nose twitched slightly before she stepped into the room, glancing about it to familiarize herself, before stepping toward the platform where upon various lengths of bandaging, body parts and empty canopic jars were placed.

Neti glanced over the body parts, before shaking her head and pronouncing, "Those can be disposed of."

"Why?" Shabaka confusedly asked.

"They were all dead, and have gone through some processes of embalming," she flatly stated, momentarily turning her gaze towards him, noticing his confusion and pointing to one of the hands, explaining, "see how the flesh has darkened on this one, this is normal for bodies having been embalmed, therefore these are not new bodies." She turned and looked at him, before asking, "Did you ever discover what happened to that body we discovered at the Per-Nefer?"

"We tracked it to the Karnak, then lost its trail."

Neti turned her attention back to the platform, silently contemplating, before stating, "If they are using bodies to move the gemstones past the guards and out of the city, it is possible that these could be some of those bodies." Shabaka looked at her in surprise, before she continued, "After they have removed the gems they would need to dispose of the bodies…the easiest way would be to throw them in the river. The river flows north and away from Thebes. Therefore, what is not consumed by the crocodiles is washed down the river."

"If they are removing the gems there, where do they hide them?" Shabaka asked, "That is what I need to establish."

Neti looked at him before shrugging her shoulders, replying, "The Karnak is almost four times the size of Thebes, with hardly any inhabitants, it is an easy place to hide. Also it would be easy to remove the gems, because there are no guards and scribes recording merchandise."

"We are now recording the movement of bodies, and we cannot deny citizens access to their gods' temples," Shabaka replied.

Neti nodded her head in agreement before extracting the scrolls from her satchel, moving off to one side of the platform and saying, "I was hoping to discuss something with you."

"What?" Shabaka asked moving closer to her side.

"Asim," Neti affirmed.

"I have men out looking for him," Shabaka quickly replied, his voice conveying his frustration.

"He's not the killer," Neti professed, unrolling the first scroll; however, Shabaka reached for her shoulders, turning her towards him before saying, "I know he was a friend of your father, and you see him as a second father, but he was in your house yesterday morning. And he could have seriously hurt you, it could have been your blood that made those footprints."

Neti lifted her hand to brush his hands from her shoulders, before turning to the scrolls, remarking, "He did not come to hurt me; he came to give me this," as she pointed to the one scroll."

"Then why the footprints?"

"He cut his feet on the pottery shards from the pot I threw at him, also his feet are the same size as mine, the killer's are larger."

Shabaka turned his attention toward the scroll, before pointing to it and asking, "What is this?"

"I have read some of it, and managed to make out dates and amounts, but I don't recognize some of the hieroglyphs, I have never seen them before," Neti said pointing to parts of the scroll.

"These are written in Nubian trade code," Shabaka said, looking at the hieroglyphs, adding, "they are records of gem shipments from the mines, with arrival dates in Thebes." Shabaka looked at her, "Where would he get this?"

"I don't know," Neti replied shaking her head.

"Then he must be involved, somehow," Shabaka said.

"I think he is scared of something happening to him or Tei-ka, that's why no one can find him."

"This shows that there is a group of people behind this…but we need to find them and tie them to the gem-filled bodies."

"This was placed in my satchel this morning when I was at the market,' Neti said handing Shabaka the other scroll.

He took it from her and opened it, glancing over the hieroglyphs, stating, "I still have trouble reading some of the Egyptian hieroglyphs."

"It's addressed to me," Neti started, taking the scroll from him. "It claims that the mayor and Ma-Nefer are involved with some scam, also that the mayor has not notified the Vizier of the murders, or some of the elder's concerns."

Shabaka remained silent for a moment before replying, "The mayor does get a percentage of the taxes, therefore he would not want to close the gates, also, I would not have wanted the gates closed until we have discovered exactly where these gems are being moved to."

Neti turned to look at the various jars, before adding, "It still does not tell us who the killer is or who are behind the gems."

Shabaka suddenly looked at her, "In that letter, they mention that Ma-Nefer and the mayor are involved in some scam; I could understand Ma-Nefer's involvement, as the body was collected from the Per-Nefer by his men and taken to Karnak. So, he could possibly be involved: in that he provides movement of the bodies."

"That does not necessarily mean he knows about the gems," Neti was quick to counter, "it is not uncommon for traders to move bodies over long distances, especially when they need to be returned to either Abydos or Aswan. We have often released bodies to traders for transportation."

Shabaka remained silent for some time, before pointing to the one scroll. "This indicates that there are gems coming in soon … and that in all likelihood those that are taken are somehow moved from storerooms to the Per-Nefer, without detection."

"The only way that would be possible is if one of the bearers or a scribe were involved," Neti replied.

"So we should be looking at the merchandize moved between the storehouses and the main Per-Nefer," Shabaka reasoned.

"That might be difficult," Neti replied, causing Shabaka to look at her in question. "Each embalmer has their own cocktail of herbs that they use when preparing bodies. These are collected whenever they are needed. Some, like my father, grow the most common ones in a communal herb garden, so that they are readily available when needed. The Natron comes from Wadi Natrun and arrives every third moon. They are not only ordered in advance, they are directly delivered to the Per-Nefer chambers, where they are also stored. Beeswax and palm-wine are both locally obtained. The only thing that is brought in and possibly stored at the storehouses is the oils used for anointing the body."

"So is there anything here that can be used to identify anyone?"

Neti looked at the jars, replying, "These we have seen before, they are similar to those used by the new embalmer. Although I do not recognize the inscriptions on them, they are not the same as ours. However, it is not unknown for the main Per-Nefer to purchase low-cost jars and oils for the subsidized funerals." Neti picked up the one jar, turning it over slightly, before looking at the body parts, "This only indicates that these were possibly state funerals," Neti said indicating to the body parts. Neti then opened the only sealed canopic jar, quickly closing it when the stench escaped, scrunching her nose before stating, "Only the minimal amount of Natron was used for preservation."

"You can tell?" Shabaka asked visibly swallowing.

"It would not smell like that if the body had been properly preserved."

Neti looked at a few more jars before selecting one, and turning to Shabaka professed, "I have seen these before. Ma-Nefer brought these into Thebes a while back. They are not proper canopic jars, but some of the private Per-Nefers have been known to use them as they are cheaper than the locally produced jars."

"So those jars can be traced back to him?" Shabaka asked.

"Only in trading," Neti replied,

"I should request a list of embalmers who he supplied with those jars, possibly search his premises to see if we find anything."

"I think you should notify the Vizier of what is happening," Neti said placing the jar back on the platform.

"Closing the gate could result in their actions becoming more desperate, most of the citizens will also object to the restrictions. Not to mention that the note will be intercepted by the mayor."

Neti looked at the one scroll, and then suddenly up at him, professing, "I have an idea, how we can bait them. It takes two days for a good messenger to reach a Vizier, and another two for him to return … that gives us four days to make this work. I need a scroll, ink and a quail."

"What are you up to?"

"We send the Vizier a message that you have discovered who is behind the gem smuggling, and will be arresting those involved in the next few days …"

"But I have no idea who is involved."

"They don't know that, and if they are involved they will panic. You then just have to keep track of their movements and arrest them when they reveal themselves."

"It might work," Shabaka replied.

Neti carefully formed the familiar hieroglyphs, and once done she waited for the ink to dry before rolling it up and handing it to him. "Here you go."

"Thank you," Shabaka returned taking it from her; I will have a guard posted close to your house, just in case."

Neti smiled, and indicated to the scrolls. "Keep them; I have no use for them."

Chapter 6

Pa-Nasi was sitting at his desk, glancing over some papers, when some commotion at the doorway drew his attention. He looked up as his house servant roughly hauled a messenger into the room, before angrily demanding, "What do you want?"

His house servant came to a halt, firmly holding onto the scrawny messenger's arm that was still struggling to break free of the man's grip.

"One of the guards caught this messenger trying to sneak a message out of town," the servant said, jerking the messenger once again to get him to stand still.

Pa-Nasi looked the man over before rising from his seat and rounding the table, haughtily asking, "Now why would a messenger wish to sneak a message out of town, I cannot help but wonder exactly to whom the message is addressed." He walked closer to the man, before lowly demanding, "For who is the message you carry?"

The messenger visibly swallowed before replying, "I cannot tell you."

"You cannot tell me," PA-Nasi snootily replied, adding, "You cannot tell the mayor of Thebes, who ensures for the town's prosperity, where you are taking that scroll." Pa-Nasi then turned towards one of his other men, commanding, "Go fetch his eldest child, so that it can receive his punishment. I hope it is a girl, I fancy exploiting the body of an innocent."

The man's eyes suddenly enlarged, giving Pa-Nasi the answer he sought, before adding, "We will see if he speaks then. If not his child will do well in the brothels."

"The message is bound for the Vizier," the messenger finally confessed, causing the mayor to look at him.

"Well now there is a problem," the mayor once again started, snidely. "For a runner may not take a message to the Vizier without my seal. Such an event is unheard of and akin to treason." The mayor stepped closer to the man before boomingly demanding, "Who sends the message!"

The runner once again swallowed, before lowering his gaze and replying, "The prefect Shabaka."

The mayor stepped back, before speaking, "Ah yes, the prefect. He dares to still challenge my authority." Then he turned and extended his hand towards the messenger, "You will hand me the message, so that I can see what is so important that he needs to directly contact the Vizier."

The messenger remained silent for a moment, and Pa-Nasi maliciously added, "I have no problem hurting your eldest, and making you watch as I do it, if you do not comply. I could even let some of my servants see to their needs."

"You cannot do this," the messenger objected.

His words saw Pa-Nasi bridging the distance and backhanding the man, decreeing," I am the mayor, I can do whatever I like!"

"No you cannot," the messenger insisted.

"Oh but I can and that is why my men will go collect your eldest," Pa-Nasi menacingly replied.

The messenger dropped his head, sighing deeply, before reaching into his satchel to extract the scroll, handing it to the mayor.

"See now that was not so hard," Pa-Nasi mocked, before turning his back to the messenger and unrolling the scroll. His brow furrowed as he read the contents of the scroll, then moved toward his desk. He rolled up the scroll and reached for his wax stick, holding it over the flame before pushing the wax over the paper and picking up his seal, and placing it over the hot wax. He then turned his attention to the messenger, saying, "It is good news, I am certain the Vizier will be pleased with his report," as he waited for the wax to cool, leaving the scroll on his desk.

"You can let him go," the mayor said to his servant, who released the messenger. He then picked up his own report to the Vizier and held it out to the messenger, "Be certain that the Vizier receives this at the earliest possible date," he said, as the messenger took the scroll from him, nodding his head in reply before turning for the door.

Once the messenger had left, Pa-Nasi turned to his footman, commanding, "Go call Ma-Nefer, I want to speak with him, now!"

The man quickly nodded his head, and turned to leave.

Pa-Nasi returned to his desk, lifting the scroll and shaking his head, pronouncing, "Fools."

The sun was just sitting above the western horizon when Shabaka arrived at Neti's home. He had finally taken up her offer for dinner, and smiled warmly when she invited him up to the kitchen.

The smell of freshly baked bread and broiling pigeon filled the air around the kitchen, assailing his senses, as Neti busied herself with their food, indicating for him to sit.

Shabaka stood for a while, looking around him, before stating, "You have a beautiful view of the city here. I am certain you could see all the way to the Rammasseum."

Neti turned to look at him, noting the direction of his gaze, before replying, "It is slightly more to the right, once the sun has set and the light is not in one's eyes it is visible."

"It must be a sight now that it has been completed," Shabaka replied.

Neti finished up and moved to stand next to him, "It is most beautiful early in the morning, but too far away to make out the precise details."

Shabaka turned to look at her, "Have you ever thought of visiting it? I would like to before I leave here."

At his words, Neti grew more reserved, and softly replied, "There are scribes working on the walls at the moment, but I would like to see it once they are done." She then turned more to the right pointing, "The Karnak is easier to see from here," she pointed toward the large building with its tall pillared entrance, adding, "from certain rooftops it almost completely obscures the view of the Rammasseum"

"You have been there?" Shabaka asked.

"Yes, every Theban will visit the Karnak at least once a year for the Opet festival," Neti replied, before adding, "the pharaoh has had many of the pillars inscribed with the history of Thebes, and his own. There are so many temples there one could not visit them all in one day. You should visit it."

"I have been within the walls, but I have never looked at the pillars or visited any of the temples. I shall have to make a point of it next time I am there," Shabaka remarked, then asked, "What are you making, it smells delectable,"

"It is just some bread and pigeon, I have not had much time to prepare more," Neti replied, then moved to tend to their food.

"That is fine with me, I would not want you to squander unnecessarily for my benefit," Shabaka replied as he moved to sit on the one stool.

"There is beer as well, if you would like some," Neti said pointing to an earthenware pot.

"That would be refreshing after today," Shabaka replied, noticing the scrolls nearby, and asking, "what are those?"

Neti handed him his beer before answering, "Those are my scrolls. I was going to go through them to try and better understand what I saw today."

"You have notes on bodies?" Shabaka asked surprised.

"Yes," Neti replied, adding, "I have compiled them since I was a child, my father often helped me. That is why everyone believes me to be a witch that can speak to the dead."

"Would you mind if I looked at them?" Shabaka sincerely asked.

"Certainly," Neti replied indicating to the scrolls, "you are welcome to."

Ma-Nefer stepped into the mayor's luscious garden. The overwhelming scent of Egyptian violets and jasmine filled the air as the skyline steadily darkened. Crickets started chirping, welcoming the cooler evening air. The last of the mayor's servants were finishing up the watering of the garden as Ma-Nefer made his way over to their appointed meeting place, watching as the mayor ordered his staff about. Ma-Nefer waited until the mayor had dismissed his staff before approaching the man, stating, "You wanted to see me."

"Yes, I did," the mayor gruffly replied, clanking about them for a moment.

His action caused a frown to form on Ma-Nefer's face, before he asked, "Why meet here?"

"Because our discussion is not for others to hear," Pa-Nasi firmly replied.

"There is a problem then?" Ma-Nefer stated rather than asked.

"Yes, and it involves the company that future bride of yours keeps," Pa-Nasi mordantly replied.

"The prefect," Ma-Nefer replied, nodding his head, adding, "yes he has proven to be a problem."

"Walk with me," the mayor commanded, gesturing to the gardens, "it will appear as a casual visit."

Ma-Nefer fell into step next to him, as he slowly started moving through the garden.

"I intercepted a message bound for the Vizier today," the mayor started, then held his hand up when Ma-Nefer was about to say something, and continued, "The prefect was sending a message stating that he has discovered the identities of those behind the gem smuggling, and that he will be arresting them in the next few days."

"Well it confirms your suspicions as to why he was sent here," Ma-Nefer calmly replied, before adding, "we have always maintained that that was the reason."

The mayor halted in the corner of the garden, and turned to face Ma-Nefer, "Yes, we have. But I had not realized that he has made any headway. I had figured with him being so occupied with the recent murders, that he would not have had the means to look deeper into the matter ... Someone has spoken, we need to find out who and silence them."

"Your embalmer perhaps, when they were there to see the mason's body?" Ma-Nefer returned, before adding, "I don't trust him, he is in too an obvious place. I told you we should put him in the abandoned Per-Nefer chamber."

The mayor shook his head, professing, "They only saw the body of the mason."

"You certain he has not said anything?"

"He keeps to himself," Pa-Nasi decreed, adding, "he knows I will have his son stoned if he does not comply."

"So what could the prefect know?" Ma-Nefer demanded, "Even those transporting the gems from the mines don't know anything. Our man at the storage facilities will not talk. My people transporting the bodies to Karnak have no idea what they are transporting, only that they are not to be unwrapped or inspected."

"Yes and that's why they killed that guard, that was a mess," the mayor retorted.

"The man should not have been as nosy," Ma-Nefer affirmed.

"What about your man at the temple who takes out the gems? He dumps the bodies, they could have questioned him?" Pa-Nasi demanded.

Ma-Nefer simply shook his head at that, before replying, "He has no tongue, he cannot speak, read or write, also he knows what will happen if he does something like that."

"We have that one body in Natron at the moment, it will only be ready to ship next week, so we cannot move it now," the mayor mused, before asking, "none of the shipments into the Per-Nefer have been checked?"

"No, everything is moved under official documentation. That Marlep is a fool," Ma-Nefer stated.

"I want to be rid of him," The mayor decreed.

"The overseer?" Ma-Nefer asked, confused.

"No, fool!" The mayor exclaimed, before clarifying, "The prefect, he has become a thorn in my side."

"Yours and mine both," Ma-Nefer deadpanned.

"It would be useful if another body could turn up with its heart removed, possibly his," The mayor mused aloud, "it would draw attention away from the gems, until we've had the opportunity to move them. But it's still a full moon's turn before the purchaser arrives from the East, and tomorrow sees the load of turquoise arrive, you know how sought after those are?" The mayor rambled.

"I will check with the others in the morning. I have stocks to draw from the storage area, and will go to Karnack with the next offerings to check on the gems," Ma-Nefer replied.

Neti and Shabaka had just finished their meal, and Neti was sitting next to him explaining some of the embalming processes, when one of the guards came into her home.

Shabaka turned his attention to the guard, asking. "What is it, Amed?"

"I have come to report that Ma-Nefer visited the mayor this evening, they were talking in the gardens," the young man replied.

"Did anyone hear what about?"

"They were too far away to hear, none of us could get close enough," Amed replied.

"I see," Shabaka answered, thinking things over for a moment before instructing, "I want both the mayor and Ma-Nefer's movements followed, I want to know where they go and who they talk to over the next few days."

Amed nodded his head in reply, before affirming, "I will have men assigned."

"Good, I want Tia-Ka brought in, in the morning. We will see if Asim reappears with his wife's arrest."

"You will not hurt her?" Neti quickly asked in concern.

"No. It's just to ensure no one else does," Shabaka replied, before adding, "Asim knows something, and I want to know what he does."

"Will that be all, Sir?" Amed asked.

"Yes thank you Amed," Shabaka replied, and with that Amed took his leave of them.

Shabaka turned to Neti, "It seems your plan has worked. If they are somehow involved they will expose themselves soon enough."

"But it still does not uncover who killed my parents," Neti regretfully replied.

"No it does not," Shabaka dolefully affirmed, "and I'm afraid that until such time as he strikes again I will not be able to do much … if only I could determine how he picks his victims."

Ma-Nefer returned to his home, and angrily stomped about the room. "That foolish mayor, it's his stupidity that has caused this," he professed aloud, adding, "I told him we should rather use the abandoned Per-Nefer chamber. No one would question an outsider practicing there, but he had to place the man at the main Per-Nefer area, had to keep things within the rules … it's time I rid myself of him as well, I do all of the work, therefore I should get all of the money."

Chapter 7

The sun was just reaching its zenith, with the sun beetles screeching in the trees from the oppressive heat, when Asim entered the guardhouse. He glanced about him, searching the room, when two guards immediately moved to capture his arms: another called for Shabaka, who soon appeared from another room.

"I want to see my wife," Asim demanded, struggling against the grip of the two guards restraining him.

"She is safe," Shabaka replied, indicating for the guards to let him go.

"She has nothing to do with this," Asim replied as he shook himself, respectively glaring at the guards next to him, before returning his attention to Shabaka.

"That is for me to decide," Shabaka calmly replied, folding his arms as he looked over the embalmer.

"She is innocent, you have no reason to keep her here, to punish her," Asim affirmed stepping forward.

Both guards moved, each taking hold of a shoulder, before Shabaka indicated to them to take him to another room.

"You can't do this!" Asim declared over his shoulder as he was forcefully escorted into a smaller room. He tugged against the two guards, turning his head to glare at Shabaka before disappearing behind the drapery.

Shabaka returned to the other room, his gaze landing on the embalmer's wife, who was seated within the one corner with Neti-Kerty.

"You are going to talk to him?" Neti asked as he came to stand by them.

"Let him sit for a while, it will cause him greater concern, make him more willing to divulge what he knows." Shabaka said, and then turned his attention towards Tea-Ka.

"You will not hurt him?" the elderly lady asked him, her tone conveying her concern.

"If he tells me what he knows, and it is not a lie, there will be no reason to have him flogged," Shabaka stated, noticing the woman's concern increase, before adding, "is there anything he would withhold, or choose not to tell me?"

He watched as she nervously fidgeted with her hands, before replying, "If there is it will be to protect me."

"And he has reason to do this?" Shabaka asked, for a moment glancing at Neti.

"No, but he has always been protective of me," Tea-ka, said before looking at him, "even if it was unneeded."

Shabaka looked at Neti, "Neti, you should come with me. I would like to know what he knows of your parents' murders. You can also act as a scribe." Neti nodded her head and rose from her seat as he continued, "I will have a guard watch over Tea-Ka whilst we are busy." He then turned his attention toward the elderly woman, commanding, "You are to remain silent, at all times, or I will have a guard move you, and he will be flogged."

Neti looked at Shabaka in disbelief as Tea-Ka quickly nodded her head.

As they stepped from the room she spoke up, "You would not really?"

"If they resist I will have no choice," Shabaka returned, causing Neti's step to falter slightly as Shabaka gathered up a few things he intended to take with him.

Neti and Shabaka entered the other room, where Asim sat on a small stool, his head lowered as the two guards stood either side of him. Neti looked him over, for a moment concerned that the guards may have forcefully silenced him, but when he lifted his head, she noticed the concern etched on his face. She reached for his shoulder before stating, "She is safe Asim."

Immediately relief washed over the man's face, and he nodded his head in reply.

Neti took a seat, accepting the papyrus scroll from one of the guards, along with the ink and quill.

Shabaka walked about the room, before signaling for the guards to step out, then looked pointedly at Asim. The man faltered slightly under his gaze, swallowing repeatedly, before lowering his head.

Shabaka held up a scroll, before harshly demanding, "What do you know of this?"

Neti immediately recognized it as one of those she had given him, and dropped her gaze toward Asim, who merely looked at the scroll before shaking his head and replying, "I don't know what it is."

"Don't lie to me!" Shabaka harshly replied, "You will be flogged for lying!" Shabaka stepped closer to the man, who cowered in response, before adding, "this is the scroll you left at Neti's home the other morning. So I repeat the question: what do you know of this?"

"I don't know anything," Asim quickly replied, looking up at Shabaka, "I could not read it, that's why I took it to Neti," he turned to look at her. "I was hoping she could make sense of it, she has always been better at reading than any of us."

"Why not take it to a scribe, or Suten Anu?" Shabaka demanded.

"A scribe would have reported it," Asim replied, turning to look at Shabaka.

"Why would you be worried about it being reported?" Shabaka demanded, glaring at the embalmer.

"All could make out was quantities and shipments. The rest was foreign to me."

"That is not reason enough to be concerned about it being reported," Shabaka firmly replied.

"It is not what it contained, but from whom it comes that had me concerned," Asim replied.

"Whose scroll is this?" Shabaka demanded.

"It fell out of one of Ma-Nefer's trekker's satchels when they were loading goods," Asim replied.

"So why not return it?" Shabaka asked looking pointedly at the man.

Asim looked at the Nubian for a while, before answering, "For years already, Ma-Nefer has made his fortune off the backs of others. At first, he started out as a shuty, trading on behalf of prosperous landowners and keeping a percentage of the goods for himself. With time, he became known for his abilities to acquire and barter almost anything. But lately very few of us are willing to do business with him."

"Why?" Shabaka demanded, "if he is so good why not use his services?"

"He has become greedy, he asks too much for his services," Asim replied.

"That is a common complain from those who want goods for cheaper," Shabaka indifferently replied.

"He has recently brought in a whole load of substandard goods, and wants top payment for it. Where some of the other shuties provide better goods at almost half the price," Asim affirmed.

"And this was why you took the scroll?" Shabaka asked in disbelief, "to see where he was cheating you?"

"No," Asim said shaking his head, before continuing, "for a while now, many of us have stopped using his services, yet the man still makes a sizeable profit. It did not seem right, especially after that time he came to talk to me."

"What conversation?" Shabaka was quick to ask, for a moment glancing towards Neti.

Asim saw the exchange and how Neti started scribing, before continuing, "He wanted to know some things about embalming and the process that it involves, as well as what we charge."

"What for?" Shabaka asked confused.

"I'm not sure, it just got me concerned, especially after the murder of Neti's parents." His words had Neti stop, and look at Asim in shock.

"What do their deaths have to do with it?" Shabaka was quick to demand, his gaze momentarily taking in Neti's disbelief.

"Neti's sudden betrothal got me concerned, there would be no reason for someone like him to seek a wife, he has slaves enough to …" Asim halted himself mid sentence before looking at Neti in apology, before continuing, "least of all one with Neti's skills."

"Why are her skills so important?" Shabaka asked confused.

"She has watched us from a young age, she knows the processes better than most, and if anyone could do something like that, it would be her," Asim replied, causing Shabaka to look at Neti in confusion, and seeing her shrug her shoulders in reply.

"Do what?" Neti asked in response, confusion clouding her voice.

"Ensure one's afterlife," Asim returned, turning to look at her. "You have always had a gift when it came to reading bodies."

Neti shook her head in response, swallowing before answering. "I have no idea what you mean by that."

Shabaka watched the exchange between them, before looking at Asim and calmly stating, "Why don't you start from the beginning, and tell us just exactly what you and Ma-Nefer discussed."

Asim looked at the Nubian, who had finally settled on a stool, looking at him, and breathed a relieved sigh before starting. "Ma-Nefer came to me the one day and wanted to know if it would be possible to ensure one's afterlife through the embalming process …"

"That's nothing strange," Neti interrupted, adding, "we often get those questions." Shabaka looked at her, as she continued, "There are many who want to know if the process has anything to do with their final judgment."

"Yes," Asim replied before continuing, "and like all embalmers, I told him that it is not the preservation of the body alone that assures a prosperous afterlife, it is the decision of the gods. And only if one's heart does not weigh equal to that of the feather of maat then Ammit will devour it, annihilating one's Ba."

Shabaka looked towards Neti who nodded her head, then returned his gaze to Asim, still uncertain as to what would have caused the man any concern, before distrustfully asking, "That was all?"

Asim sighed dejectedly, dropping his gaze to the floor, then shook his head before answering, "He asked then if it would be possible to switch hearts during preparation process."

"What!" Neti replied in disbelief, before adding, "That's sacrilege! Switch hearts! Who would even think of such a thing?"

Asim lifted his gaze to look at her, before replying, "That's what I thought, but he seemed taken by the idea, professing that if it all depended upon the weighing of the heart then having a pure heart would ensure an afterlife, and that one could charge whatever price one wanted to for that."

"And you agreed to it?" Neti asked in disbelief.

Asim simply shook his head, "It would take a highly skilled embalmer to do such a thing, if they even were to attempt it, and even then, they could lose their papers if it was discovered. I do not know of one embalmer that would chance doing something like that."

"And you told him as much?" Shabaka calmly asked.

Asim turned to look at Shabaka, replying, "There's no reasoning with Ma-Nefer when his mind is set, and I did not think anything would come of it until Neti's parents were murdered."

"Because their hearts were removed," Neti spoke up, nodding her head slightly.

Asim once again acknowledged, before murmuring, "That, and the fact that you are now betrothed to him."

Shabaka cleared his throat, causing both of them to look at him, "The only problem with that is we know that he did not kill Neti's parents, a beerhouse owner said he was there discussing business with some men."

Asim remained silent for a while, his head shaking almost imperceptibly, before replying, "It would have been the beerhouse on the south side of Thebes."

Shabaka looked at Asim, before getting up, saying, "It was, so you are either lying to me, or not telling the whole truth. Either will result in you being flogged."

Asim sat back suddenly, looking fearfully up at Shabaka, stuttering, "I can explain."

"You better, because I don't take kindly to being lied to," Shabaka seethed, noting Neti's cautious glance at him.

"I know he was there because I saw him," Asim quickly replied, "I usually go there for a beer before returning home."

"So why imply that he killed Neti's parents?" Shabaka asked moving behind Asim so he could not see him.

"I did not," Asim started turning to look behind him, his voice already fearful, adding, "he sneered at me whilst they were discussing something and looking over some scrolls. I thought that that was one of them," he said indicating the scroll Shabaka had left next to his stool, adding, "and that maybe it could help Neti get out of her marriage."

Shabaka remained silent for some time, causing Neti to turn and look at him. Asim nervously fidgeted, and finally tried to look at Shabaka.

"Are you familiar with the new embalmer Karendesh?" Shabaka finally asked.

"I have seen him with Marlep but I have not spoken to him, he keeps to himself."

"So you know nothing about his embalming?" Shabaka asked, looking over the man's head at Neti, silently commanding her to remain quiet.

"I would imagine they were the same as any other embalmer's, maybe with the exception of the usage of herbs," Asim replied, giving a slight shrug.

"Has Ma-Nefer ever approached you to process any bodies?" Shabaka asked, placing his hands on the man's shoulders, causing him to startle and quickly reply, "No."

"Not even his slaves?" Shabaka asked, tightening his hold slightly, causing Asim to cringe.

"No. They are buried in the desert, like the others. There is no preparation for them."

Shabaka looked over to Neti, before asking, "And your father?"

Neti simply shook her head in reply, and continued with her scribing.

Shabaka then moved from the man before collecting up the scroll next to his seat, asking, "So you have no idea what this is then?"

"I could only tell dates, and quantities," Asim replied.

"As could Neti. It was written in Nubian," Shabaka dismissed, then demanded, "Why were you avoiding us?"

Asim visibly swallowed before answering, "Ma-Nefer is a vindictive man. He was already angered that we had placed our requests for fabric with another shuty, and if I was seen talking to you, knowing what I know … if he had anything to do with the death of Neti's parents, there would be no reason for him not to kill me and my wife as well."

Shabaka nodded at that, but noticed how Neti's gaze dropped, and softly asked, "Neti?"

She looked up at him, then shrugged her shoulders, "All this time I was wondering why my father would do business with Kadurt, why he would be willing to accept the man's money, and if he did where would it have gone, and now I know."

Asim looked at her frowning, "What money?"

"My father would have used the money to buy fabrics; he knew how much my mother liked to make clothing. He could never deny her anything."

"What does Kadurt have to do with it? I admit, yes, your father did order some fabrics for his Per-Nefer and your mother, but he would never be foolish enough to do business with that man," Asim replied confused.

"But he claims that I owed him a hundred and twenty Debben," Neti replied.

"Your father was not foolish, he would never have made such debts, as your mother gave up her favorite amulet as part of the payment."

"We need to speak to Suten Anu," Shabaka replied, looking toward Neti, who in turn was looking at Asim in disbelief.

"The Purity of Heart amulet that Tea-Ka wears is my mother's?" she asked in disbelief.

"I could not part with it, for I know how much it meant to your mother. But after your father paid the application fees for your certification, and Ma-Nefer demanded upfront payment for the natron, your father did not have enough money to purchase the fabrics. Your mother offered her amulet, as payment toward the fabrics."

"But you kept the amulet?"

"As security. I paid in the difference. I had intended to return it once your mother had made some dresses and could repay me the amount. But instead they were murdered," the last was said in a very dejected tone.

"And you gave the amulet to Tea-Ka," Neti replied, before stating, "I would like to buy it back. You can have anything you want, I would like for her to be buried with it."

"You should discuss it with Tea-Ka, but I will first have to explain to her where it came from."

Shabaka cleared his throat, causing both of them to look at him, stating, "We should go Neti."

"Can I see my wife?" Asim was quick to ask, his voice hopeful.

"No, Sit tight," Shabaka commanded in return, and Asim's shoulders drooped.

Neti followed him from the room, holding the scroll open to allow for the ink to dry, then looked at him in surprise when he commanded two of the closest guards to bring in Kadurt and his men. Shabaka then turned to one of the Captains, and ordered an increase of their surveillance of Ma-Nefer and Pa-Nasi, and that any meetings between them be reported, that included messengers.

Neti was just starting to roll the scroll, when two young recruits came into the guard house, reporting that Ma-Nefer had earlier been seen talking to a specific scribe at the stores, while his men were loading.

Shabaka instructed them to discover the man's identity and to report back, before sending another recruit to summons Suten Anu.

The three-quarter moon had just risen above the horizon when he made his way along the somewhat crowded road in the more affluent side of Thebes, where most of the inhabitants were making their way to some engagement or other. Their preoccupancy with their own matters ensured his anonymity, especially since his dark clothing portrayed him as a foreigner, and one with whom few would associate. He glanced across the road, silently cursing the amount of guards present. The previous evening had been similar, and it had been difficult getting close enough to enter the house.

He tugged his knife back into place under his cloak as he slipped down the one side road. A person moving in the opposite direction bumped into him, causing him to hiss slightly, cursing his human body and its limitations. He continued up the road before slipping through a hidden entrance, glancing around again before making his way along the wall.

He approached the opulent house with ease, then looked about again, ensuring that there were no guards moving within the premises before entering the home, hissing again as he bumped his knee clambering through the window.

He glanced around the darkened room, the servants had retired for the evening and he carefully stalked through the house. He glanced about looking for a suitable object; he could not bring his club, it would have drawn too much attention. He finally found a throwing stick, and he swung it a few times to see how it would handle, before gleefully grinning, thinking that he only needed a few more hearts then he too would be a god. This man was appointed by the pharaoh, and had a position of power over people: he needed that power, and would take it with his heart.

He carefully approached the man's bedroom, slowing when he heard the low grunts emitted within, knowing that the man was rutting. Many women willing to rut with him, women who liked his power: it was another thing he coveted the man as he slipped into the room.

The man was naked, gripping the young woman by her hips as he jerked against her, his movements fast as he grunted with effort. He fought against his desire to watch them, his own body responding, especially to the young woman's moans – although he was not certain if they were due to pleasure or pain, her body jerked as the man thrust into her, repeatedly.

He lifted the throwing stick and stepped closer, the man was too preoccupied with his actions to even glance about him. He brought the stick down hard on the back of the man's head, causing the man to jerk suddenly before dropping to the ground. The young woman jolted in shock, and turned to look at him, her eyes suddenly enlarging. As he stepped closer, his attention drawn to her body, his desire to rut with her was overwhelming. However, the woman opened her mouth: screaming. Her action snapped him out of his lust-induced stupor, causing him to once again hoist the throwing stick, knocking her out as well.

He glanced about, moving into the shadows to see if anyone came looking, and then when nothing happened returned to the two bodies, well aware that the staff had been taught to turn a deaf ear to any screaming originating from the man's bedroom.

Shabaka was sitting at his platform, looking over the scrolls under the lamplight, when a young recruit came bolting into the guardhouse, announcing through panted breaths, "There was a scream at the mayor's house."

"That is not unheard of," one of the guards blithely replied.

"It was not a pain-filled scream, it was one of terror," the young recruit professed.

"Has anyone entered the premises?" Shabaka asked rising from his stool.

"Not through any of the gates," the young recruit said.

"We'll go see what's up anyway," Shabaka said stepping around his platform, when one of the guards ribbed him, "Leave it. The man is obviously rutting one of the young slave girls, they tend to scream the first time, wouldn't want to be interrupted if I were him."

Shabaka looked pointedly at the man, before gesturing toward Neti-Kerty and Tea-Ka whom were present in the room. The guard shrugged his shoulders, replying, "They are old enough to understand."

"That they may, but it does not excuse bad manners," Shabaka reprimanded the man, before adding, "you can remain here with the embalmer and his wife, we will go see what is happening at the mayor's house." Shabaka ushered Neti to accompany him. "

They entered the mayor's estate, silently approaching the house. Shabaka glanced about, and sent a few of the guards to collect the servants, for a moment wondering if they were not overstressing the situation.

If there was any problem, none of the servants seemed perturbed when the guards ordered them out, simply shrugging their shoulders when asked about the scream.

"They don't seem too concerned," one of the guards spoke up as they looked over the group of servants.

"I don't think they really want to know," another close to Shabaka replied.

"Who sees to the master's rooms?" Shabaka asked glancing out over the group.

A few indicated to a young woman, who finally stepped forward and meekly replied, "I have been charged with that duty."

Shabaka looked at her for a moment, before asking, "Is there anyone with him this evening?"

The young woman looked about her for a moment, ringing her hands before nodding her head, "Yes, a young woman."

Shabaka looked at her, wondering just how young the woman was, before commanding, "You will take us to his rooms."

The young woman looked about to protest, then simply agreed, replying, "This way."

As they neared the bedroom, the familiar copper tang hung in the air, causing Neti and Shabaka to look at one another. Shabaka pulled the servant back, indicating that she be silent and to return to the others, assigning a guard to accompany her.

They watched as they left, then visibly steeled themselves for the scene they were about to enter, as they stepped past the rich drapery.

Neti halted dead in her tracks, feeling the bile rise in her throat as the man crouched over the woman lifted her still beating heart over his head. A delirious giggle escaping his lips, as the blood ran in rivulets down his forearms.

"Thoth!" she exclaimed in disbelief, shaking her head slightly in denial.

He turned his head to look at her, and she felt a bolt of shock jolt through her body, immobilizing her to the spot. Even Shabaka seemed shocked. Neti felt her knees quake as the realization struck that her best friend had ... that she had cleaned his hands afterwards ... that he had ...

Thoth looked at her for a moment, his face lighting, until he recognized the man standing next to her and swore under his breath. He leapt from his position and ran for the window scurrying through it, clasping the heart in his one hand as he landed outside. He glanced around, looking to see where the other guards were before setting off for the secret entryway.

Shabaka leapt forward in the hope of catching the man, however he halted on reaching the window, it was too small for him to pass through. He turned towards the others, commanding, "Catch him! Don't let him get away!" They turned to look at the scene before him: the young woman's chest was hacked open, her blood lying in a pool around her, whilst the mayor lay motionless to the one side. He moved over to the mayor then turned his gaze to Neti, calling, "Neti. Neti!" the second shout releasing her from her stupor, as he continued, "Can you tell me if he is alive?" indicating the naked body before him.

Neti looked towards it and then turned her gaze away, causing Shabaka to look down at the body, noting its condition before realizing why she had averted her gaze. He pulled a sheet from the bed and covered the lower region of the man's body, before once again calling her to have a look.

Neti stepped closer, mumbling, "Now I've seen more of him than I care to."

Shabaka smiled in response, before answering, "You should be used to it by now."

Neti sank down to her haunches, before replying, "I am. But there are some things in life that are best left unexplored." She placed her hand on his chest, adding, "His body is one of them."

She tilted her head slightly and moved her hand a bit, waiting a few moments before she raised it, holding it over his mouth. "He is alive," she finally noted, adding, "not awake, but alive."

Shabaka nodded in response, stepping past her toward the door, "I'm going to see if they caught him," adding, "I will have a healer sent for," then he disappeared behind the drapery.

Neti looked around the room, noting the amount of blood, and the trail of bloody footprints, and swallowed.

Shabaka momentarily reappeared in the doorway, calling, "Neti," causing her to turn and look at him, before asking, "You okay?"

She regarded him for a moment, almost nodding her head in reply, but then at the last moment shook it, shrugging her shoulders.

"We'll get him," Shabaka professed. Neti merely inclined her head in response.

Shabaka had just stepped from the house, when one of the guards approached him, "I don't know how he got away, but we cannot find him. There are too many dark places for him to hide." The other guards then joined, awaiting instructions.

"Take some of the men and search Ma-Nefers's property, everywhere, including the trading post. I don't care who is woken or disturbed. If there is a problem, detain them. We must find him." Shabaka watched the man go, then turned to one of the recruits, "Go summons Suten Anu, tell him his assistance is needed here," before looking at the recruit next to him, "go summons a healer. The mayor is still alive."

Both turned from him, setting off as fast as they could, before he returned to address the others, commanding, "I do not want any of the elders on the property. You two will seize all documentation you can find, have the scribe go over it," Shabaka added, pointing to two men in the group, adding, "I will tell him what to look for once he gets here." The men nodded and moved toward the house.

Shabaka then looked toward the one recruit, commanding, "Return to the guardhouse and have them prepare my chariot, then have it brought here." The young man nodded his head before turning and setting off. He then pointed to another group, "You four, make for the gates and tell the guards that no one is to leave Thebes until I say so." He then turned his attention to the rest, "The rest of you keep people out of here," he ordered before returning to enter the home.

He entered the room a short while later, finding Neti carefully stepping along the bloody footprints. He watched her for a moment, before speaking up, "He managed to get away, but the guards are out looking for him."

Neti nodded her head, and turned to look at him when his hand gently landed on her shoulder.

"You okay?" he asked.

"I'm not sure," she honestly replied, shaking her head.

Shabaka squeezed her shoulder gently, and she offered him a weak smile in response.

Just then, a healer entered the room, his eyes bugging at the scene before him, exclaiming, "By Amun-Ra! What happened here?" He finally turned to look at Neti and Shabaka, nodding in greeting, before carefully moving to the mayor's side and checking the man's vitals.

"You should send for Marlep, and have her body removed," the healer said, indicating to the young woman.

"I'll send someone," Shabaka replied, before turning to Neti, beckoning, "come, I have sent for Suten Anu, you could possibly help him go over the documents, you do not need to be here now." He returned his attention to the healer, "I will have a guard sent, to ensure that you are not disturbed."

The healer inclined his head in acknowledgement, replying, "He can help me move him onto the bed then."

Thoth once again checked over his shoulder, wanting to ensure that he was not being followed: knowing it would only be a matter of time before they discovered his means of escape, and would then follow him. He needed to get back to the chamber, he would be save there, and no one would think to look for him there.

He slipped down the narrow alleyway, once again glancing behind him before moving down it and stepping into the chamber. He moved over to the platform first, placing the heart on it before he returned to the door to collect the lamp. Striking the flintstone, he lit it and moved it into position; he gathered up everything he needed, the familiar feeling of power filling him as he once again picked up the heart, holding it over the basin so he could wash it with the wine.

From a darkened corner, Ma-Nefer watched as Thoth processed the heart, smiling in glee. He dropped his voice as he asked, "You have taken the heart requested?"

Thoth halted for a few moments, looking around him, before answering, "No."

"What!" Ma-Nefer demanded, stepping closer, "Then whose heart is that?"

"The girl's," Thoth gleefully replied, "Neti found me before I could take his, and that dark man was with her."

"You were supposed to take the mayor's heart, not some slave girl's!' Ma-Nefer started, lifting his hand, and then suddenly realizing he did not have his whip with him, fumed. "You useless piece of flesh."

"I did not have time," Thoth calmly replied as he placed the heart in the jar, causing Ma-Nefer to look at him in disbelief.

"But you killed him?" Ma-Nefer demanded

"I do not know," Thoth replied reaching for the natron and filling the jar.

"You fool! Do you know what you have done! They now know who you are! They are going to come looking for you, and they will kill you!" Ma-Nefer lividly exclaimed, adding, "I'm now going to have to move the gems, before their location is discovered!"

Thoth looked after Ma-Nefer as he left the chamber, then glanced at the jar before him, placing the lid on it before following the man, thinking that as a god he had right to all the gems: he was not going to let this man steal them from him.

Back at the mayor's house, Suten Anu periodically glanced sideways at Neti: after his arrival and their disclosure of events, he had kept her close to him and ensured that no one disturbed her. Her head was down whilst she scanned scroll after scroll, casting some aside and adding others to a small pile.

Shabaka was pacing, irritable, and periodically glanced towards Neti, before resuming his pacing.

A short while later, one of the recruits entered the room, breathing hard. "A traveler was seen to be moving along the northern road towards Karnak, he is bulky and appeared to move with haste," the recruit reported between gasps, and then bent forward struggling to regain his breath.

"No one travels in the dark," Suten Anu replied. "It is to easy to fall prey to vagabonds and bandits."

"Unless you are on of them, and trying to hide something," Shabaka replied, turning to the one guard, commanding, "ready my chariot, call together as many men as you can and follow." The guard nodded his head in reply, and left.

"Take Neti with you," Suten Anu said as Shabaka prepared to leave.

"It is too dangerous," Shabaka replied, shaking his head.

"If it is Thoth, he will listen to her, and come to her if she calls him," Suten Anu explained, "He always has."

Shabaka looked towards Neti, then acknowledged, beckoning, "Come, we must go."

Shabaka and Neti stepped out of the mayor's house, Neti halting at the sight of the two gray horses, stepping back as one tossed its head and the other snorted before pawing the ground.

"Come they will not hurt you, they are well trained," Shabaka replied, guiding her round the horses. "I forget that Egyptians are not yet used to horses."

He indicated for her to step onto the chariot, and she looked at the half-round carriage with its overly large wheels in suspicion.

"It is safe, and much faster than running."

Neti swallowed hard as she got on the platform, immediately stepping back when she saw the horses' quarters, her body slamming into Shabaka's as he too stood on the carriage. His arm snaked around her holding her in place, assuring, "Relax You will be fine." He then collected up the reins and commanded the horses to set off.

The cooler evening air blasted across Neti's face as the horses cantered along the road, kicking small sand and stone particles that stung as they struck her skin. Her eyes watered from the unaccustomed wind force.

Shabaka's arm tightened around her as the horses turned the corner. The sudden jolt as the chariot once again straightened had her yelp slightly; her gaze dropped to the pair of quarters before her, causing her to pinch her eyes shut and visibly swallow, whilst pushing back against Shabaka: her heart pounding as fast as the horse hooves seemed to.

Dogs and cats scattered to get out of the way, and citizens that were still about turned to look at them in disbelief as the chariot rushed past them, and on towards the Northern Gate.

Shabaka checked the horses as they approached the gate: the guard already moving into position to detain them, until he recognized the chariot and the occupants and moved out of the way.

"Close the gates after the guards, no one leaves!" Shabaka commanded as they passed, before turning his attention back to the road.

A short distance from the gate some hyenas scampered over the road, barking excitedly as the horses rushed past.

On Shabaka's command, the horses once again sped up, and Neti, who had not thought they could go any faster, gripped the frame of the chariot so hard that her knuckles turned white.

The chariot bumped and jolted as they made their way along the dirt road, only slowing slightly as they crossed the bridge over the channel.

The horses' hooves continued to mercilessly pound the moonlit road, diminishing the distance between Thebes and the Karnak.

Shabaka steered them away from the Avenue of Rams, past the entrance to the Opet Temple and onwards to the Avenue of Sphinxes that led towards the forecourt of the temple of Amun-Ra.

He checked the horses again; bringing them down to a trot as they turned onto the sandstone path, slowing them, their hoof beats sounding sharper on the hard surface. The chariots movements suddenly smoothed, causing Neti's grip to loosen, as she watched the horses as they pulled the chariot up the slight incline.

Entering the first pylon, the sound of the horses' hoof beats became overwhelming, filling the walls with a hollow clonking sound. The smell of horse-sweat filled the air, with the horses breathing hard as they continued on to the forecourt. The hoof beats again altered, this time echoing off the vast walls, with the horses snorting loudly and tossing their heads.

Shabaka again tightened his arm around her before asking, "Where do you think they would go?"

Neti looked about the large courtyard noticing how the lamps around the forecourt flickered faintly, the light playing on the nearby carvings. "I don't know," Neti finally answered before asking, "did your men not follow them the last time they came?"

"They were only recorded entering, the guards were not allowed to interfere with proceedings."

"I see," Neti thoughtfully replied, adding, "it's difficult. There are several temples here, all devoted to different gods, unless one knows which divinity they came to worship, there is no telling. They also got a head start on us,"

"Horses travel faster than humans; if they came to collect the gems then they should still be here."

Shabaka halted the horses near the Ramesses statues, leading into the second pylon, and got off the chariot, stating, "Come, we'll search for them on foot, the horses will alert them of our whereabouts and make it easier for them to avoid us."

"The horses will not run away?" Neti asked in surprise.

"They have been trained to stand," Shabaka replied, looking about the area, adding, "we should go see the priests, they may have heard or seen something."

Neti nodded her head and fell into step beside him, looking about them, then suddenly reached for his arm, "Shabaka, look!" she gasped, pointing in a direction.

Shabaka peered into the direction she indicated, and tried to see what she was referring to, when he finally made out a dark shape moving along the wall, almost undetected.

"Halt!" he ordered, "in the name of Rammeses the Second I command you to stand."

The figure halted, and Shabaka jogged over to where he stood. He looked at the dark cloak then lowered his head to address the man, "Father."

"What is it you seek son?" the man asked, his voice low and calming.

"I seek the man who came this way; I need to know if you have seen him."

"I may have, but what could you possibly want with him? He is one interested only in power, it will be his downfall. Surely you, who has a noble heart would not seek out such a person."

"He has done great injustice to the pharaoh, I have been sent to collect him."

"And your friend here, what is her purpose?"

"Father I do not have time, the man I am looking for has killed several and taken their hearts, I must put an end to it."

The priest looked at him for a while before answering, "Whilst doing my evening rounds of the temples, I noticed two men enter. One from the South Gate, he went to the sacred lake to wash. The other entered through that gateway." The priest indicated the pylon they had entered through, "And went into the Hypostyle Hall."

Shabaka looked towards Neti for a moment before stating, "Thoth would have gone to the lake, it will be a while before the guards arrive; we should seek Ma-Nefer first."

Neti nodded her head, and followed him back to the second pylon, to move through it and on to the Hypostyle Hall.

The lamps along the main pathway were all lit. The colossal pillars rising up to the ceiling were covered in colorful hieroglyphics that seemed to come to life in the flickering flame. The pillars beyond those were all cast in shadows. The hall was eerily silent, only the sound of their footsteps could be heard as they moved along the passage.

The sudden fall of footsteps in quick succession had Shabaka halt, his hand going out to still Neti's progress, whilst he intently listened to the sounds. Neti's heart started thumping in her chest as she also listened, trying to make out the direction.

"Ma-Nefer?" she whispered.

Shabaka shook his head, before drawing her with him into the shadows, before whispering in reply, "The footfalls are too light and too swift for someone large."

"Thoth?" she then asked, her heart pounding against her chest, as she glanced about them.

"Possibly. I'm trying to determine where he is."

Neti remained silent, listening with him, her throat dried, and she swallowed repeatedly at the lump that had formed there. She clasped her hands that had started sweating.

The footsteps echoed again and Neti looked at Shabaka, unable to make out his features fully in the dark. She whispered, "If it is Thoth, he will come if I call."

"And if it is not, and Ma-Nefer is within these walls, it would forewarn him," Shabaka firmly replied.

"You could easily outrun Ma-Nefer," Neti professed, "he knows that."

"That is also why he would not run, but slink away like a snake in the reeds. We have to determine in which direction the person is moving."

Neti released a heartfelt sigh and remained silent for a while. She looked up at Shabaka as his hand gently landed on her shoulder.

"I do not know if the man wandering through these pillars is the same person as the one you know as your friend," Shabaka softly stated, "I cannot risk that he suddenly becomes deranged and attacks you."

"Thoth will not harm me," Neti said confidently.

"How can you be so sure?" Shabaka lowly demanded. "He killed your parents!"

Neti stiffened at that, swallowing visibly as she clasped her hands, before stepping away from him and back into the light, saying, "I will just have to find out." She called, "Thoth! Are you here?" Her voice echoed through the hall causing her to turn around in confusion.

"Neti?" Thoth replied, his confusion evident in his voice, adding, "You should not be here."

"Thoth, come out, come to me," Neti called again looking about her when the only response she got was more footsteps sounding. Her heart thudded against her chest as she looked in Shabaka's direction.

"You have him with you!" Thoth angrily stated, the sound once again bouncing off the walls, making it difficult to determine exactly where he was. "He is in the way, he needs to be taken care of."

"Thoth, this is not you, come out," Neti implored, again glancing around, his footsteps no longer audible. She glanced toward Shabaka's direction, her heart pounding in her chest, as a sense of dread flushed over her. Thoth may not hurt her, but he would Shabaka and she did not want that, had not wanted any of this.

Thoth's voice was clearer this time, "No! He interferes. He needs to go. I cannot become a god, until I have his heart."

"Thoth this is nonsense, come on out," Neti said, turning into the direction the voice appeared to come from; peering into the shadows, Shabaka also looked about.

"He has to go, he cannot have you," Thoth shouted.

"Thoth, please come out. As your friend, your sister, I'm asking you to come out and talk to me."

"He has claimed your heart, he cannot have it. You cannot help me if he owns your heart, that is why I must take it."

Neti could feel the anger rise in her, never having thought anyone would notice her partiality to Shabaka. However, Thoth would have been the most likely to notice, having always been the one closest to her. She turned to look around her, the echoing within the hall made it difficult to discern his whereabouts, at times the footfalls sounded as if there were two moving about. She clenched her fists in an attempt to control her anger, before challengingly replying, "Is that why you killed my parents?"

"They separated us, they took you from me," he angrily accused, his voice sounding closer, adding, "I have to right it, we have to be together, you will make me a god."

Neti just shook her head at that, taking deep breaths to calm herself, before replying, "How is killing those I love correcting a mistake?" she felt Shabaka's eyes bore into her back at that, but chose not to acknowledge it.

"They cannot have you!" he stated. His voice was clearer, with less of an echo this time. Neti felt her heart race as her mouth dried. She glanced at Shabaka, then at the area immediately surrounding her.

Neti cleared her throat, swallowing a few times before suggesting, "Come out Thoth, so that we can talk. You can tell me why you had to kill them,"

She felt her heart drop as his crazed giggle reached her ears, followed by, "You are in the precinct of the temple of Amun-Ra. I too will soon be a god like him. The prefect is nothing to you. He is in the way, and needs to go."

Neti glanced at Shabaka who had also been looking around, he whispered in reply, "The guards will be here soon, we only need to keep him here until they arrive."

Neti nodded her head, and then firmly said, "That does not mean you need to kill him Thoth."

"He was chosen by the pharaoh, he holds a position of power, I need that."

Neti no longer knew what to say, and hoped that the guards would soon arrive, as Thoth had sounded really close. However, she could not make out anything in the shadows as she peered into them. She looked toward Shabaka and was about to open her mouth to pre-warn him, when Thoth struck.

His angle was off, hitting Shabaka on the shoulder instead of over the head. A sickening cracking sound came from Shabaka's shoulder, moments before he bellowed in pain.

Shabaka turned toward his attacker, barely able to make out his shape in the dark, and ducked the second blow. He moved quickly to swipe Thoth's feet from under him. The man landed with a resounding thud, scampering back onto his feet as Shabaka reached toward his left shoulder, gasping in pain as the bones within moved against each other.

Thoth collected up the broken torch he had been using, growling, "You will die and I will be a god," before taking another swing at the prefect.

Shabaka avoided the blows, and tried to close the distance between them, wanting to rid Thoth of the torch, wanting to level the playing field; however he found it difficult, especially with the throbbing of his shoulder.

A scream from the side caused him to look toward where Neti had stood, moments before, and saw her being dragged off by Ma-Nefer: kicking and struggling against the man's hold. He turned to follow her when Thoth again swung the torch, this time striking Shabaka across his stomach, just below his ribs: Shabaka grunted as he doubled over, coughing.

Neti watched as Shabaka doubled over, and shouted at Thoth to stop, doubling her effort to break loose from Ma-Nefer's unrelenting grip.

Ma-Nefer smacked her hard, causing her head to snap back from the momentum, resulting in Neti's vision becoming a sea of spots..

"He's as good as dead," Ma-Nefer professed. "Thoth will kill him, so shut up and come with me."

"No! I will never go with you," Neti avowed, once again renewing her struggles, "I would rather die."

Ma-Nefer tossed her down to the ground, and kicked her hard a few times. Her head eventually struck the stone floor, knocking her unconscious, before he tossed her over his shoulder and started for the northern exit of the hall.

Thoth had the torch up against Shabaka's throat, pushing down against it with all his might, whilst Shabaka tried to throw the man off him, his injured arm throbbing, impeding his ability to successfully knock the man from him. He grunted and groaned in his effort as Thoth sneered over him, "She is mine, you will never have her. But I will take your heart."

Shabaka started seeing black spots, gasping for air as his arms and feet started flaying. His vision started blurring whilst his heart rate increased. Thoth's crazed giggle, the glee he could hear in it, had him renew his efforts, intent on protecting Neti from these men.

His arms and body became slack as he stopped fighting. The sudden change and his stillness caused Thoth to lessen the downward force of the torch against his neck, allowing him to catch Thoth off-guard. He suddenly kicked up, twisting firmly to one side, grinding his teeth against the pain that shot through his shoulder, and managed to throw the slave off him, rolling clear, gasping for breath.

Thoth landed with a loud thud. The fall alone would have winded most, but Thoth and was surprisingly strong for his size, and capable of taking a considerate amount of physical punishment. He simply rolled over and snatched up the staff, before regaining his feet and returning to where Shabaka was kneeling, still gasping for air. Thoth lifted the torch, preparing to strike, and Shabaka barely managed to roll out of the way, the blow striking the ground a few inches from him.

Shabaka again tried to regain his feet but Thoth kept on striking at him. His shoulder was throbbing, and he yelped in pain when he accidentally landed on it. He turned onto his back, intent on easing the weight off it, when he saw Thoth's crazed expression, it forewarned him that there would be no sense from the man. He knew of Neti's bond with Thoth and would have settled for simply capturing him. However, the man held no similar sentiments towards him, and continued his merciless assault. His single blow once again struck Shabaka's injured shoulder, causing Shabaka to bellow in pain, his right hand instinctively reaching for it, as it hung limp from his shoulder.

Thoth took the opportunity to knock him to the ground, again strangling him with the torch. This time Shabaka knew there was no way he could fight off the man again, his vision once again blurred, his body sore, beaten, yet his heart still sped up in defiance.

There was a scuffling sound not far from them, and Shabaka at first thought it was Ma-Nefer, who had returned to help Thoth. When the voice of a young recruit, through his gasps for breath commanded, "Let him go!"

Thoth only giggled in response, before pushing the torch down even more.

The young recruit then rushed forward, knocking Thoth off Shabaka, causing the slave to tumble a short distance. The recruit righted himself and moved toward Shabaka, not noticing that Thoth had regained his feet and taken up the torch.

Shabaka, through his coughing and gasping, tried to warn the young man, however Thoth was too swift, swinging the torch with practiced ease, hitting the young recruit on his neck. The cracking sound and the way the man lifelessly dropped to the ground was enough indication to Shabaka that the blow had been fatal.

Shabaka knew the rest of the guards would not be far behind, but as he looked at the rage on Thoth's face, he doubted they would be in time. He once again tried to rise from his position, however his body resisted, and Thoth, high on adrenaline and glee, yanked the young recruit's body out of the way as he approached.

Shabaka knew that Thoth was beyond reason, beyond the point of feeling any pain: he had seen soldiers in a similar trance on the battlefield, how they displayed almost superhuman strength.

Thoth once again went for his throat, this time with his hands, "I will watch you die," he grunted as his grip tightened.

Just then, two more guards arrived and noticed Shabaka's predicament. Without any hesitation, they attacked the slave. The first made to grab him, however Thoth caught him at the optimum moment, using the guard's momentum to toss him against the one pillar. The guard dropped to the ground and made no attempt to move. The second managed to pull Thoth off Shabaka. However Thoth in his grazed state turned on him, going for the man's face and catching him off guard, forcing the man back against one of the pillars: smacking the back of the man's head against the sandstone pillar. The guard slipped to the ground without resistance as Thoth let go of his face.

Thoth turned back toward Shabaka, just as the armed guards arrived. The men took in the scene before them and lifted their spears. Without mercy, they attacked, stabbing the slave several times before he dropped to his knees.

"The gods will strike down all of you. When I join them I will ensure that your families carry the burden of your actions," Thoth yelled, moments before one of the guards delivered the final blow.

A bulky guard, who Shabaka knew as Asis, knelt next to him, helping him up, whilst the others checked on their companions.

Once Shabaka found his voice, he commanded, "I want this place closed off, not a person enters or leaves!"

"But we have captured the man," the guard replied in confusion.

Just then, one of the others asked, "Where is the woman?"

"Ma-Nefer has her," Shabaka returned, adding, "I want every palace, every corner of this place searched. Guards at every gate. We have to find them."

He then attempted to regain his feet when Asis halted him, placing a hand on his bruised chest, stating, "You need to see a healer."

Shabaka brushed off the man's hand, hissing when it bumped his left arm, averring, "It can wait until we have found Neti."

Asis turned toward the arriving guards, commanding, "Guard all the gates. No one enters or leaves, the rest of you pair up and start searching the temples."

Chapter 8

Ma-Nefer, huffing and spluttering, dragged Neti's unconscious body down the darkened passage. The loud scraping sound of stone on stone indicated the closing of the doorway as he progressed down the narrow passageway. He knew it would not be long before the guards would start searching the palace. The discovery of Shabaka's body would leave them hungry for blood, and they would be after Thoth in full force, and with their attention focused on him, it would give him some time to escape once the sun had risen.

The passageway eventually opened up into a lit chamber, and he gave one more heave, before letting go of Neti's limp body, leaving it to lie there. He moved toward the bags stacked along the far wall, grabbing the first, undoing the rope before reaching into it, extracting a piece of turquoise and smirking as he ran his fingers over it: it was the most sought after gem, only the pharaoh and his family wore it. The bag alone was worth a small fortune.

He returned the gem to the bag, and lifted it to estimate its weight, before looking at the other bags. There were fourteen in all, each one containing the gems of two bodies. He returned up the passage, placing his hand on the raised stone that would trigger the release mechanism for the stone door, and waited as the door once again scraped open, looking about once it had done so.

He knew that off to the left was a series of stalls, where he would fine a donkey or mule, and made towards it.

It was deadly quiet in the precinct of Montu, and he continued to glance about, knowing it would only be a matter of time before the guards made their way there. He walked through the stall finally loosening the lead rope of a large mule and a donkey; he would make Neti walk as soon as she had woken. He took a pack harness for the donkey, tossing it over his shoulder as he led the two animals back to the entranceway, chasing the donkey ahead as he tugged the mule along, once again pressing the stone and waiting for the entrance to close.

The mule nearly stepped on Neti as they entered the chamber, swerving to avoid her, and received a hard jerk from Ma-Nefer in return. He checked over the animals, they were well cared for: and in his opinion overfed, as all animals belonging to the temples usually were.

He tacked up the donkey, ensuring that the cinch wad was firmly tightened, before starting to load the gems onto the animal's back, securing the bags into place.

A short while later, a moan from the passage had him leap around, only to release a grunt when he realized that it was Neti, regaining consciousness.

He smiled as she grunted in pain, clasping her head between her hands, thinking to himself, that will teach her to listen.

Neti-Kerty righted herself, her body felt tender and ached in objection to her movement, her head pounding as she swallowed down the bile rising in her throat. She glanced about the area unable to remember how she got there, or what she was doing there, and shook her head in an attempt to clear the fuzziness, immediately hissing as the pain in her skull intensified. She looked about the room, and finally identified Ma-Nefer, for a moment watching as he loaded a donkey.

She tried to rise, however the spinning dizziness in her head soon had her sink back down to the ground, clasping her head as the shock on the impact jolted through her. She gasped for breath in order to control the pain.

She had another look around her, needing to identify her surroundings, and then took a deep breath and shouted, hoping someone would hear her. She knew Ma-Nefer would in all likelihood beat her for it, but the guards should have arrived.

"You can scream all you want, no one can hear you," Ma-Nefer sneered as he secured the last bag.

"Someone will!" Neti remarked, moments before letting rip yet another scream.

"This is the treasure chamber of Amenhotep the third, no one will hear you."

"That is only a myth. No one has ever discovered it," Neti quickly countered, panting for breath as the pain once again took hold.

Ma-Nefer just sneered at her, "Foolish woman." He then commanded, "Come, on your feet," as he grabbed her by her arm and yanked her upright.

Neti felt her head spin at the sudden change of position, her stomach also revolted: causing her to doubled over, heaving harshly as its contents were expelled,

The acid smell filled the musty chamber, causing her to hurl again.

Ma-Nefer instantly let go of her arm and she staggered for a few steps before managing to brace herself against the wall.

"You're pregnant with that bastard's child!" he professed looking at her.

Neti lifted her head, for a moment trying to figure out what he meant, when a thought struck her, causing her to reply, "What if I am?"

Ma-Nefer growled at that before shortening the distance between them, backhanding her across the face and causing her to once again sink to her knees.

"You are useless to me, I can't have any sniveling half breeds running about, they are useless you stupid woman. I cannot even sell a half breed!" he affronted.

Neti tried to rise, but her body felt too weak, sickened further by his words.

"You might as well stay here and die, for you are of no good to anyone," he returned, before kicking her in the side, hard.

Neti grunted against the pain that shot through her body, folding in on herself, hoping it would lessen the pain.

Ma-Nefer then turned from her, once again chasing the donkey ahead of him up the passageway, yanking the mule behind him.

When he got to the top, he opened the doorway and glanced about, before allowing the animals to exit, closing the chamber once again.

It was as he was clambering onto the mule that he noticed the guards' entry into the precinct from the southern entrance, their white clothes made them easy to spot in the fading moonlight. He swore under his breath as he turned the mule toward the gate, pulling the donkey along as he whacked them on their quarters, causing them both to shoot forward in response; the mule staggering slightly under his bulk, almost unseating him. They trotted down the avenue of sphinxes and turned right, heading east.

He made it to the nearest underbrush before returning his gaze back toward the gate; he urged the animals off the road slightly as he watched the gate. It was only a while later that two guards took up their positions there.

He knew that there was no way they would discover her or the secret chamber, and turned his attention back to the path he was cutting through the wild vegetation.

Shabaka was hobbling on the southern side of the temple on Amun-Ra near the sacred pool. One of the guards had tied his arm to his body, making it almost impossible to move, and he winched slightly as he slowly moved about.

There had been no word yet; the guards were still searching the grounds, when one of the herders approached him, "Prefect Shabaka," the man hesitantly started, already causing Shabaka's heart to drop, knowing the news could no be good.

"Yes," Shabaka replied, turning to face the man.

"There is a donkey and mule missing from the stalls," he hesitantly continued, then added, "The guard said I should report it to you."

"Where!" Shabaka demanded.

"They are kept in the Precinct of Montu."

"Take me there, at once!" Shabaka instructed and then walked as speedily as he could toward the temple.

He was almost faint with pain, and covered in a sheen of sweat when they finally stopped at the stalls. He gasped as he fought the darkness threatening to take hold of him. Bile rose in his throat at the sight of the two empty stalls, knowing there would be little chance of catching them then.

Shabaka braced his good shoulder against the post of the stall, breathing deeply as his eyes closed; he was tired, most of the men were tired, there was no way that they would give chase, not after having been up the whole night.

The guards guarding the precinct came closer, the one speaking to the herder before helping Shabaka upright, and commanding one of the others, "Go fetch his chariot, we need to get him to a healer."

In his pain-filled haze, Shabaka's gaze landed on a dark skinned man, dressed in the robes of the western barbarians. He peered into the distance, noticing how the man beckoned him to approach.

Shabaka pulled his good arm from the guard holding it, and blindly started in the direction. The guard grasped at his arm and he tried to stop him, looking around to see what had captured his attention, but failed to notice anything.

A new sheen of sweat started glistened on Shabaka's brow as he neared the area where the dark skinned man stood, tilting his head slightly, when the man's foreign accent reached his ears, "That what you seek is beyond the wall."

The guard looked about in concern, especially since there was nothing there, and Shabaka seemed to look intently at one place.

"Follow the footsteps. What you seek is closer than you think, but farther that you can imagine."

Shabaka shook his head, drawing in a deep breath and lowering his gaze to the ground ... when he saw it – animal tracks.

He lifted his head suddenly, the action left him slightly light-headed as he sought out the dark figure, but it was gone. Lowering his gaze again he started following the tracks, the guard moved to catch up with him and was about to say something when he noticed the trail Shabaka was following, one that led directly to the wall.

Shabaka halted at the wall, the hoof prints seemed to both disappear and reappear from the wall, the one area well trampled.

Shabaka turned to the guard, weakly commanding, "Get the others to follow that, see where it goes," before turning to the wall, mumbling, "beyond the wall."

He looked closely at it, his pain-dazed mind finding it difficult to concentrate on things. Eventually he rested his forehead against the wall, trying his best to keep his footing, when a man in one of the temple's robes took his shoulder, drawing him back. Some of the guards rushed towards them, then halted in amazement when the man placed his hand on the one brick, pressing it and moving his foot to put pressure on another brick.

The heavy sound of stone scraping against stone was heard as part of the wall before him moved, revealing a sloping passageway. Stale air billowed out, carrying with it a slight acidic smell. Shabaka peered down the corridor, lamps low along the passageway burned with renewed vigor as fresh air flooded the chamber.

He turned to two of the guards and gestured for them to investigate; both were hesitant, causing him to demand, "What's wrong?"

"We have no desire to die," the one answered.

"What do you mean?" Shabaka demanded in disbelief. "It is part of the temple, it cannot be cursed."

"Those who do not know the password on return will be killed," the other remarked.

Shabaka turned to the man who had opened the doorway.

"Is it true?" he demanded,

The man shook his head in reply, causing Shabaka to frown, before asking, "Why do you not speak?"

The man gestured with his hands to his throat, making a funny sound, causing Shabaka to nod his head in understanding, "You have no tongue." He then turned towards the men, ordering them to enter the passage or risk defying an order, and they relented, both cagily entering the passageway, whispering to each other to look out for traps.

A short while later they called back, "We found her!"

Shabaka felt relief wash over him, before calling down to them. "Good, bring her up."

The two guards appeared a few moments later with Neti suspended between them, moaning in pain.

"Neti?" Shabaka gasped, alarmed by the limpness of her body, and the blue marks around her mouth.

"Need air," she panted as they lay her down on the ground.

"Just breathe," Shabaka replied, becoming calmer when he noticed the color slowly dissipate.

Just then the guard appeared with Shabaka's chariot, and Shabaka turned to look at it, before addressing those remaining, "Gather the fallen ones, I will send out others to follow the trail," before indicating to the guards to help Neti on the chariot.

Neti-Kerty shook her head when she realized what they were doing, stating, "No I'm not well enough to go on that."

"We will go slow," Shabaka professed, as they placed her on it, adding, "Just sit."

"The temple have offered an oxen and dray to convey the others," the one guard reported.

"Then gather up the fallen and let's return them home, the killer has been stopped, they have done well," Shabaka professed before stepping onto the chariot. Taking up the reins in his good hand, he asked the horses to move on, and slowly they made their way back to the city.

The guards at the North Gate stood at attention as the dray approached, opening the gates when they recognized the chariot, and lowering their heads as those having fallen passed them, the others waiting respectfully behind the dray.

"The gates are open," Shabaka said, as they moved past the guards, "The murderer has been found."

The guard nodded his head, "I'll send my recruit right away."

Children playing in the street stopped and stepped out of the way, many of the citizens stopping to look as the procession past them, all lowering their heads in respect.

The dray altered course, turning towards the main Per-Nefer Chambers with half of the guard following, whilst Shabaka, Neti, and remaining guards continued onto the guardhouse.

Suten Anu, Asim and Tea-Ka were outside the guardhouse waiting, the message of the returning guard having swiftly moved through the streets.

Shabaka halted the horses and slowly stepped from the chariot, and indicated to the chariot when Suten Anu hastily approached him.

Neti moved a little, dangling her legs off the end of the chariot as she tried to gather together the strength to stand up.

"Neti," Tea-Ka gasped when she saw the condition of her and the bedraggled state of her clothing, "are you okay?" the woman asked, rapping her arm around the girl's shoulder, to which Neti hissed, "I'm sore."

Tea-Ka looked towards Asim, instructing, "Go find a healer, now!"

Neti made to protest, but Tea-Ka would have none of it, telling her to stay put until the healer arrived.

"Neti," Suten Anu softly spoke, causing her to look up at him, "you might want to have a look at this," he pulled out a scroll.

"Neti carefully took it and unrolled it, starting to read. Tears formed in her eyes as she read the document.

"Neti?" Shabaka asked in concern, "What is it?"

"My papers, they confiscated my license," she replied the tears running down her cheeks, "they would have done anything."

Suten Anu cleared his throat, causing her to look at him. "We also found something else," he started, watching as she cocked her head slightly. "Your parents' hearts."

Neti's eyes bugged at that, her jaw slacking as she made to ask, but was too scared to.

"They were placed in canoptic jars with natron. Asim said they are well preserved and that they can be returned as soon as the bodies are removed from the natron."

Neti smiled through her tears.

Suten Anu then turned to Shabaka. "There were gems found in some of the grain sacks, and have been gathered up and placed in a basket for safekeeping."

"Good," Shabaka replied, leaning slightly against the wall.

"We are making an inventory of everything that has been collected ..." Suten Anu started, then suddenly halted, when Shabaka stumbled slightly, instead professing, "come, the two of you need to see the healers."

Epilogue

Neti-Kerty carefully walked along the road, wincing slightly as her brimming satchel bumped against her still bruised hip. She held the urn of anointing oil close to her breast as she passed a group of children, who were merrily playing in the street with a goat bladder ball. She stopped for a moment to watch them, before continuing along the road toward Asim's chamber.

It had been several days since their return from the Karnak, and it amazed her how quickly the atmosphere within the city had altered: she was not certain if it was the citizens' relief that the killer had been stopped, or the fact that the mayor was finally being held accountable for his actions.

It had also been several days since she had last seen Shabaka. However, she knew that with the completion of his obligations he would soon be leaving, and thought it best to avoid him. The thought of his leaving caused a heavy sensation to settle over her heart, and she tried not to think about it. She had enjoyed working with him; it had tested her skills, her ability to understand the bodies she looked at …

She chided herself, it was an important day, and she should not ponder on such trivial thoughts. She drew in a deep breath, and pushed the thoughts to the back of her mind once she arrived at Asim's Per-Nefer chamber.

Asim greeted her at the doorway, taking the satchel from her, before leading her into the chamber.

"That will be your platform," he said indicating to the one on the far side.

Neti walked over to it, carefully placing the urn of oil on it, before taking her satchel from him. She unpacked the bandages and amulets she had brought to one side, placing the folded clothing next to that, followed by her father's embalming tools.

Asim stood watching her as she prepared, smiling faintly as she laid out her things in the same meticulous order her father used to.

Just then, the bearers arrived with the first, neatly wrapped, cadaver, and placed it on the platform she was to use, before retreating to collect up the second. Asim handed her the measure of spiced palm wine and indicated to the large earthenware pot, and she nodded her head in response.

The bearers brought in the second body, placing it on Asim's platform, before leaving the chamber.

Asim handed her a canoptic jar, which she took and carried with the utmost care toward her platform, placing it next to the carefully folded clothing.

Neti turned to look at Asim in question and he nodded his head, before she started unwrapping the cadaver, brushing the natron from it and revealing the darkened flesh beneath it. Neti fell into the familiar routine: open a section; scoop up the used natron; drop it in the large earthenware pot, before repeating the whole process to reveal the body beneath it.

She looked down at her mother, before turning to look towards Asim, who was working on her father, sincerely stating, "You have done a wonderful job, Asim, " whilst indicating her mother's chest, and his reconstruction work.

"Reconstruction was always your father's strongest skill," Asim replied as he continued to clear off the natron.

Neti took up her the flint knife and severed the stitching on the left flank, carefully placing it back in its place before pulling out the stitches. With great caution and meticulous care she started to remove the temporary stuffing and dropped it into the earthenware pot.

Once completed, she brushed the last of the natron from the body, cleaning off every trace, finally closing the earthenware pot once she was done. She drew a smaller earthenware bowl closer, decanting some of the palm wine into it, then set about washing the body. Her precise, yet practiced strokes removed the remaining natron, and she took extra care to clear all of it from the body. She finally collected up the canoptic jar, opening the lid and pouring off the excess natron. She extracted the heart within and carried it over to the bowl of palm wine, tenderly washing the natron from it, before returning it to the body.

Neti emptied out the bowl of palm wine, collecting up another bowl, before making her way to the sawdust and filling the bowl: then returned to her mother's body to do the final packing. She carefully filed the area surrounding her heart, packing the body tightly, and finally reached for the needle and thread to re-stitch the cut, before sealing it with resin.

After packing away everything she no longer needed, she reached for the urn of anointing oil she had specially made for her mother, having scented it by adding oil from her favorite flowers. She poured some into her hand, rubbing her palms together, before starting on her mother's body. Her touch was gentle, as she meticulously worked the oil over the body; the measured strokes and repetitive action calmed her. Once she had finished, she reached for her mother's favorite dress, and carefully redressed the body.

She had just finished when Asim called her, "Neti," causing her to turn and look at him. "There is a parcel for you at the shelves," he said, pointing to a small parcel wrapped in fabric.

Neti walked over to the shelf, picking up the small package and opening it. Her breath caught, and she swallowed at the lump that had suddenly formed in her throat. Her eyes started burning as she tried to contain the tears threatening to spill.

"Tei-ka said it would only be proper for your mother to be buried with it," Asim professed as he continued his own work. Neti again swallowed and nodded her head in response, unable to find her voice. She lifted the amulet from its wrapping, and returned to her mother, placing the amulet around her neck.

Asim left the chamber for a few minutes, before returning with the bearers: carrying a pot with warmed bees' wax.

"Bees' wax?" Neti asked in disbelief, knowing only the wealthy landowners and pharaohs had their bandages coated with bees' wax.

"Only the best for your parents. They were friends in the truest sense of the word," Asim avowed as the bearers carefully situated the pot.

Neti took the first of the bandages and started wrapping the body, placing the amulets within the carefully sewn pockets: she had made them exactly the way her mother used to.

Once the body was wrapped, Neti reached for the first of the final layer's bandages, dipping it in the wax, allowing the waxy liquid to permeate the fabric before lifting it out and proceeding with the final layer: repeating the action with every subsequent bandage.

She finally moved her hands over the bandaged body to smooth out any wrinkles that had formed.

A tingling sensation started along her spine as she finished, with a tremendous sense of pride filling her. She frowned at that, for pride was not the proper emotion to feel at that moment.

She looked up, seeking out Asim, when she saw the translucent, ghostlike images of her parents: both standing a short distance from her.

Her father had his arm wrapped around her mother, and both of them were smiling at her. There was a young dark-haired boy with them, who waved at her.

She swallowed repeatedly when she recognized that the clothing they had on were those they had just been dressed in. Her mother's amulet hung around her neck and there were no visible marks on her father's chest, unlike those found on his body.

A great sense of calm overcame her: the knowledge that their hearts had been returned to them, as she had avowed, eased her burden. She was filled with a warm sensation, one she could only justify as her mother's love, before they disappeared from view.

"There now," Asim spoke up, drawing her attention back to the present, "They are ready for the progression, and the opening of the mouth ceremony."

Neti nodded her head, then started cleaning her area.

That evening she sat down to dinner with Asim and Te-Ka, sharing stories of her parents.

The following morning, Neti took up her position in the procession, surprised by the number of attendees having arrived to escort her parents to their final resting place.

Suten Anu took his position next to her, with Asim and Tei-Ka walking behind them. Neti glanced about, and was surprised when Shabaka joined the procession: his arm was held stationary and bandaged to his body, and he still walked with a slight limp.

She had dinner with Suten Anu a few evenings prior, and he had filled her in on the proceedings, informing her that Shabaka was finalizing the arrangements for his departure. Also, that Shabaka found himself dealing with an ever-increasing amount of complaints the citizens were logging against the mayor.

Neti's attention returned to the present, as she slowly walked behind the bier, until it came to the graveside. The priest performed the Opening of the Mouth ceremony, and the bearers moved the sarcophagi from the bier to the grave: placing them next to each other and carefully placing the canopic jars with them.

Neti approached the grave, placing her mothers gardening tools and sewing equipment next to her, before turning to her father, placing the Senet game and his collection of amulets beside him. She then stepped back and allowed the gravediggers to close up the grave, remaining until they were done.

She felt his presence behind her, long before he spoke up, "You think they will be happy?"

Neti looked up at the sky, smiling as the sun warmed her skin, before replying, "Yes, they will be fine." Thinking it better not to tell him that she had seen their spirits. She turned to look at him before sincerely asking, "How have you been?"

"Busy," he flatly replied.

Neti nodded her head slightly, and then replied, "Suten mentioned that you are keeping him busy, he almost missed our dinner the other evening."

"He is a very competent man," Shabaka replied before gesturing with his uninjured hand for her to join him, adding, "Come, I will walk you back."

"So how are things, really?" Neti asked, falling into step next to him.

"Difficult," Shabaka replied, then elaborated when Neti looked at him, frowning, "The complaints against the mayor are constantly increasing, I had hoped that we would be done already, but they just continue to come in.

"He was not the honest man he portrayed himself as being," Neti stated, adding, "most of us knew you could pay him to turn a blind eye."

"You have a complaint?" Shabaka was quick to ask.

Neti gave a slight shake of the head, answering, "No, other than my license papers, I have avoided the man."

"I see," Shabaka replied, and then continued a short distance before he asked, "how are things?"

Neti smiled before replying, "Much better since we returned. I'm not fully accepted, but at least not everyone seems set on avoiding or insulting me."

"That's good,"

They walked some distance further,, and Neti's heart started racing as the city gates loomed ahead. Finally out of desperation she asked, "Have you heard anything about Ma-Nefer?"

Shabaka looked at her for a moment, "No we have not seen hide or hair of him, but the guard is to be notified the moment he enters town. We have also sent word to Abydos and Aswan, who should he be headed in that direction."

"And the exchange that Suten discovered?"

"The guards will go out and arrest anyone that shows up, however I think that a man with Ma-Nefer's cunning would not be as foolish."

"I see, and Kandurt?" she asked as they entered the Eastern Gate.

"He and his men are still missing. They must have cleared out of town within moments after Suten paid him; possibly fearing the repercussions of their actions."

"And the mayor?"

Shabaka audibly sighed at that, "The mayor refuses to talk to anyone, said he will plead his case with the pharaoh."

Neti huffed in disbelief, "I doubt that the pharaoh would listen to him."

"That is debatable," Shabaka replied, as they turned onto the road her home was situated on, finally asking, "what are you going to do now?"

Neti smiled at him, replying, "I, am going to prepare lunch," hoping she could get him to join her.

"No," Shabaka quickly replied, "I didn't mean right now. I meant now that everything has come to a close."

"Oh! Sorry," Neti replied, her heart suddenly feeling heavy. "Marlep offered me the remaining chamber at the main Per-Nefer; until I am able to continue on my own."

"I see, so you will continue your family heritage," Shabaka replied in a low tone, giving a nod of his head, his gaze dropping to the ground.

"It is what I know, and I'm good at," Neti deadpanned, adding, "And you?"

"I have to escort the mayor to the Palace," Shabaka said as they halted before her home.

"I see," she replied, "I take it you will be leaving soon."

"We're leaving in the morning; the barge is being loaded as we speak. I did not want to miss your parents' funeral."

"Thank you," Neti mumbled in reply.

Shabaka cleared his throat, "Also, I wanted to come see you."

"To say good-bye?" Neti questioned.

"Not quite," Shabaka replied, taking a deep breath, before once again clearing his throat. "I came to ask you if you would be willing to accompany us to the palace." Neti looked at him in surprise, causing him to quickly add, "I realize that you have plans. However, you helped me to capture him, and the pharaoh would want an audience with you."

Neti looked down at the ground for a moment, a tightening sensation started squeezing at her heart, "And that's all?"

Shabaka remained silent for a while, causing Neti to look up at him, before he replied, "No. Not really." His reply had Neti tilt her head slightly, her heart speeding up at the thought that he might be interested in her, her heart once again shriveling when he replied, "I was hoping that you would consider joining up with me. I know it's a big decision, and you don't need to answer now. You can wait until we have seen the pharaoh and finished this. But I could really use your skills. You see things, understand things and think differently than the others. You make comparisons, and deductions, and I need that if I'm going to continue with this."

Neti swallowed, before asking, "And where would we do this?"

"Wherever the pharaoh sends us," Shabaka keenly replied.

"I see," Neti drawled.

"Please just think about it. I could really use your help, and there's nothing binding you at the moment," he quickly replied, then suddenly having realized what he had implied, added, "Is there?"

Neti shook her head, "No, but I will have to make arrangements. I cannot just leave everything unattended."

"I will help," Shabaka was quick to volunteer.

Early the following morning, from the reeds next to the river, Ma-Nefer watched as they boarded the barge bound for the Palace, along with the mayor and guards, sneeringly vowing, "I will get you for this."

Neti-Kerty and Shabaka return in

Princess of Egypt

The Mummifier's Daughter - Book 2

Prologue

A BROWN FISH EAGLE hovers in the cloudless sky, its wingtips playing in the breeze as it floats almost motionlessly above the Nile, waiting for the fish to surface. Below, crocodiles sun themselves in the morning sun as wild Egyptian geese and white cranes wade through the reeds in search of insects and plant bits.

Water splashes against the sides of the wooden bark as the river's current conveys it on the final leg of its journey toward the new capital city, having departed from Memphis at first light.

Neti breathed a sigh of relief. Their journey had taken longer than she had anticipated, with a string of delays having hampered their progress; the mayor's failed escape attempt and the subsequent loading and off-loading of the bark had only served to irritate her.

She stood as far up the prow as she could and gazed out over the water. Her white slip moved gently in the slight breeze and provided some respite from the oppressive humidity that shrouded the bark. Earlier, there had been children playing along the river's edge, with women doing their washing. Though the farther they moved into the delta, the fewer humans they encountered.

Turning to look back at the men, she listened as Pa-Nasi once again complained about his treatment, with the bark's captain mumbling something vile in response. She, however, only shook her head when she heard something along the lines of "bloodying him and throwing him to the crocodiles." The captain had not been welcoming of the disgraced Theban mayor and made no attempt to hide his animosity toward Pa-Nasi, which had made the journey to Pi-Ramesses tortuous.

Neti had opted to remained distant from the men, especially since a few of them had leered at her in an impious fashion. Though they had treated her no differently than any of the others onboard, she preferred to keep to herself.

Shabaka's arm was still in a sling, and as she glanced over at him, she could not suppress the strong sense of agitation that came over her. When they had embarked on their journey, she had hoped that his insistence for her to accompany him implied interest. However, since their departure, he had not given her any clear indication of what his intentions were or whether he even had any. Her attraction to him had only grown, and she was uncertain whether it was because of his attentiveness toward her or his insistence that the others should respect her.

She had on occasion caught him staring at her, appearing to be deep in thought, and though she knew she was different from the other women in Thebes and that her origins could not be fully traced, she had hoped he would at least look past that. She was not obtuse; she knew he held a position of rank, which alone implied that he derived from upper class descent, possibly close to the pharaoh.

He appeared more at ease the closer they came to the new city, and it gave Neti a lingering suspicion that not everything was as it appeared.

In many ways, she was thankful that they were to moor the following afternoon, because she felt an oppressive need to place some distance between them, if only to organize her thoughts, for it was difficult to remain aloof while they shared such a confined space with the others.

Chapter 1

RAMESSES THE GREAT was seated in his assembly hall with all his advisors when the gilded doors opened and a young messenger came running into the hall. The young man dropped down on his knees before the pharaoh and bowed his head, wheezing as he awaited acknowledgement.

"Yes, Moses, what is it?" the pharaoh calmly spoke, his voice not as strong as it had been all those years ago.

"My gallant Lord," the young man spoke between pants, "the bark from Thebes has arrived."

Ramesses looked at the young man before speaking. "Are the prefect Shabaka and the embalmer's daughter on it?"

With his head still lowered, the young man replied, "Yes, my Lord."

"Good." The word sounded more like a sigh of relief. "Return to the waterfront and inform him that I wish to see both of them, immediately."

"Yes, my Lord." The young man rose from his position and firmly nodded before turning to leave the room. Ramesses watched as the young man set off once again at a hard pace, and for a moment he envied him his youth and vigor.

"You cannot mean to have her enter here!" an overly obese man close to him said. "You have heard the reports about this woman."

"Reports from whom, may I ask, Khay? The very mayor they have captured stealing from me?" Ramesses reproached the vizier. "His word carries no weight anymore. He has proven himself a thief, and we all know that thieves are also liars."

"But surely you cannot allow a tainted one to enter the house of a god," Sahure, the treasury advisor, said, *"for it will certainly bring misfortune to the kingdom."*

"I will do as I like. This is my home you speak of, thus my wish to have her here. So I will not care for another word to be spoken about it."

Those surrounding Ramesses nodded their heads and looked among themselves, exchanging concerned glances.

A short while later, the great doors to the hall opened again to admit a small group of people, with two of the palace guards bringing up the rear.

Ramesses looked them over, his gaze moving from the mayor and the men walking with him to Shabaka and the petite woman who walked next to him. He was taken aback by her appearance, and his gaze remained fixed upon her as they approached him. His mind flirted back to when Maathorneferure had been such a captivating young lady, for she had looked strikingly similar, with the same delicate face and fine lips. However, Neti was still too far from him for him to see her eyes, but he imagined they would be as expressive as Maathorneferure's. Hittite women were strong, honest, and loyal to their men, and he could understand his prefect's enthrallment.

The group came to a halt not far from him, and Shabaka knelt, with Neti-Kerty and the others following his example. The mayor remained defiant until one of the guards smacked him with a staff, and then he too finally sank down to his knee and lowered his head.

"Rise, my prefect," Ramesses spoke, *"for you have served me well. Word has traveled of your deeds, and of those who have helped you."*

Shabaka rose and looked at the god-king.

"You too, Neti-Kerty," Ramesses said, and he watched as she rose to her full height, almost a full head shorter than Shabaka, and lifted her gaze to meet his. Her eyes were the eyes of her people, clear and expressive.

His gaze moved toward the mayor, who had attempted to rise only to have the guard once again push him down.

"I believe, Shabaka, that you have brought before me the person responsible for the pillage."

"From the records we recovered, my Lord, it is apparent that his was the mind behind it."

"And the other one?"

"He escaped capture, my Lord, but they are seeking him."

"And I am certain he will be captured," Ramesses spoke, turning his attention to the mayor. *"It appears I may have been deluded by your loyalty, Pa-Nasi, and that I have chosen a quisling and a thief to care for the old city in my absence. For even with the knowledge that disloyalty to either me or Egypt is punishable by death, you have heeded the words of the gods of greed and sloth. You chose to steal from your king, and for that you will be suitably punished."*

Pa-Nasi made to speak up but was silenced by the guard, who once again whacked him with his staff, harshly commanding *"Do not interrupt the Pharaoh!"*

"A charge of defiance shall be added to those of theft and betrayal. And, if found guilty of these charges, you will be flogged forty times before being placed in the lion's den," the pharaoh continued, undeterred by the man's insolence as he turned toward his vizier. *"Khay, does he have any kin?"*

"No, my Lord, none that are known of," the corpulent man replied.

"Then his punishment will remain on his shoulders alone," Ramesses concluded, and indicated for the guards to take him and the others away, leaving only Neti and Shabaka before him.

Once they had left the room, he returned his attention to Shabaka. *"My prefect, you spoke of records; I expect you to produce these."*

"I have handed them to the young slave you sent to meet us."

Ramesses nodded in reply. *"Yes, he is one of my most loyal,"* he said, before turning toward the men gathered around him. *"Homer, I know that he would have taken the documents to your office. I want you to go over them and report back to me, tonight."*

"Yes, my Lord," a tall, refined man spoke before rising from his seat. *"If you will relieve me of my duties here I shall tend to the matter immediately."*

Ramesses dismissed him before demanding *"Where is Nebty? For she will have another to attend,"* while he looked at Neti.

"I have been told that she has left the palace to see to her family," Khay replied.

"Then who, pray tell, is tending to my daughter?" Ramesses demanded, turning to look pointedly at the man.

"One of the palace servants, my Lord," Neferronpet, Khay's assistant, replied.

Ramesses' gaze returned to Neti. "I apologize, my dear, for not only have the tales of your beauty done you injustice, it seems that the palace is not properly prepared to receive you."

Neti remained silent for several moments, glancing at Shabaka before replying "Thank you, my Lord" and inclining her head.

Ramesses in turn glared at those around him before indicating them to leave. Once the others had left, he released a relieved sigh and turned his attention back to Shabaka and Neti. "They become more bothersome by the day," he pronounced, and then looked from one to the other, wondering how truthful the rumors of them were.

He focused his attention on Shabaka. "I trust your family will be happy to see you again," he said, and as he spoke he noticed how Neti's body immediately stiffened, the action quickly followed by a startled sideways glance.

"As I will be to see them," Shabaka replied sincerely.

"I expect you desire to return to your quarters and rest after your journey. Therefore I will detain you no longer, but I expect you to join us to break bread this evening."

Shabaka lowered his head in acknowledgement. "As you desire, my Lord."

"I will have your companion shown to her quarters as soon as a servant arrives."

"That will not be needed," a calm yet firm voice from the side said, causing everyone present to turn and look in its direction. The queen had entered through one of the side doors, dressed in the sheerest white gown Neti had ever seen. Her gold necklace was emblazoned with turquoise stones and a lined sash hung from one shoulder. She gracefully moved farther into the assembly room, as if floating.

Shabaka quickly dropped down on one knee, and Neti, enthralled by the woman's presence and carriage, followed her progress as she approached them.

"Maathorneferure, my queen," Ramesses said as she came to a halt near Neti. His voice snapped Neti out of her stupor, and she quickly knelt before the queen.

"My Lord," the queen replied, and then looked at the woman before her, whom she addressed in her native tongue. But Neti did not respond. She spoke again, this time her tone harsher, and still got no response. "I see you do not speak Nesili," Maathorneferure spoke finally, causing Neti to look up at her. "Perhaps you have been in Egypt too long to remember any."

Neti simply looked at the woman, her uncertainty written clearly across her face.

"Rise, young one, you are to come with me," Maathorneferure said gently. "Do not let these men and their ways overawe you."

Neti rose from her knee and brushed her slip back into place. She had not had the opportunity to clean up since their arrival, and her appearance was unbefitting the privilege of being the queen's escort.

"My queen," Ramesses spoke as Maathorneferure turned to leave.

"She will remain in the care of my servants, that way I can forewarn her of the intentions of palace men, and the attentions of a Pharaoh," Maathorneferure teasingly returned.

"As if I see any other for you," Ramesses was quick to riposte.

"And what of your other wives, you tell them the same?" she playfully challenged him.

"That I do not, for you are my primary and most loved," Ramesses professed with his hand over his heart.

"Be that as it may, I understand your attentions better than most, my Lord," Maathorneferure quipped teasingly before leading Neti from the room.

Ramesses turned toward Shabaka once they were alone. "You have chosen well, but I am not certain whether you have yet won her heart or her loyalty. If she is anything like my wife, you will have a difficult time convincing her of your affections."

Shabaka nodded before he spoke. "Thank you, my Lord."

"I trust you have not told her of your family or your origins." Shabaka shook his head in reply. "Then I will not demand your presence at court until such time as you have."

"Thank you."

"Go, rest. You deserve it."

We hope you enjoyed this excerpt from

Princess of Egypt

The Mummifier's Daughter - Book 2

Available now.

Made in the USA
Lexington, KY
14 April 2019